and
TERRIFY
PEOPLE

# HOW TO
# MAKE A

### and
# TERRIFY
## PEOPLE

Alette J. Willis

Floris Books

FOR LAURA

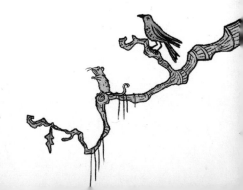

Kelpies is an imprint of Floris Books

First published in 2011 by Floris Books
© 2011 Alette J. Willis

Alette J. Willis has asserted her right under the
Copyright, Designs and Patent Act 1988 to be
identified as the Author of this work.

The publisher acknowledges subsidy from
Creative Scotland towards the publication
of this volume.

British Library CIP data available
ISBN 978-086315-840-7
Printed in the UK
by CPI Group (UK) Ltd, Croydon

# HOW IT ALL BEGAN

Mum led the policeman into our house but I wasn't ready to go back in yet. I stayed in the front yard, watching as my whole world pulsed blue from the lights on the police car.

A gust of wind blew through the woods behind the house, rustling through the dry leaves. It sounded as though the trees were whispering to each other. I shivered, wrapping my warm coat more tightly around me.

As the wind died down again, I heard a new noise: a faint *squeak, squeak, squeak,* growing louder as someone or something came up the road towards me. I peered into the night. All I could see were the lines of houses on either side of the road, their windows curtained and dark, and the empty pools of light cast by the streetlamps.

The noise grew louder, crawling up my back like the sound of fingernails on a blackboard. I clamped my hands over my ears. Just when I thought I might scream to drown out the noise, a boy appeared out of the gloom. He was riding an old-fashioned bicycle, one of the ones with big springy seats and high handlebars, a Mary Poppins bike. Every time his feet went round, the wheels protested: *squeak, squeak, squeak.*

The boy stopped behind the police car and stared at me, his owlish eyes unblinking behind his round glasses. He was about my age, tall and skinny. His thick black hair stood up from his head, like he had a really bad case of static electricity, and none of his clothes fit right. The trousers were too short for his long legs and his jumper hung around him like a tent. He looked like someone who would get picked on at school. I would have felt sorry for him, except he was staring at the police car, my house and me with such greedy curiosity, I decided he probably deserved whatever he got. I hate it when people act like someone else's problems are entertaining.

I scowled at him. He blinked, put his feet on the pedals and cycled away, disappearing into the shadows without a sound.

"Edda, aren't you coming?" Mum called from the front door.

I walked slowly across the yard, dreading going back inside and having to face the wreck the burglars had made of my birthday presents.

"What were you staring at?" Mum asked as I stepped through the doorway.

"The boy on the bike," I said.

Mum looked confused. "What boy?"

"The one who stopped in front of our house," I said, equally puzzled. "You must have heard him. His wheels were making a horrible noise."

Mum shook her head and gave me a small, sad smile. "My mind must have been somewhere else."

I left my coat in the hall and followed her into the living room where Dad and the police officer were waiting.

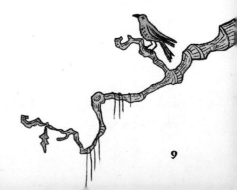

# 1. COMING HOME

The day everything began to go wrong started off well. It was my thirteenth birthday and Mum made my favourite breakfast: pancakes with maple syrup. At school, Mrs Doak got the class to sing Happy Birthday to me, which none of the teachers at my previous schools had ever done. It made me feel like grinning with pleasure and crawling under my desk in embarrassment all at the same time. But what made that day better than any other birthday was that for the first time I had a best friend to celebrate with.

Some people keep diaries. Me, I keep a sketchbook. So as I walked home from school with Lucy Chu, I was thinking about the picture I would draw later when I was alone.

First, I'd sketch Lucy and me striding down the leaf-covered pavement in our matching navy skirts and jumpers, strands of mousey brown hair blowing about my freckled face, Lucy's black hair staying in its tidy bun despite the wind. Then I'd add the sun shining down on us, bright yellow in a blue sky, and Corstorphine Hill in front of us, gold and green trees at the top, rows of houses snuggled against its slopes. My house stood up there. Since it was near the top, all I could see from the main road was a corner of its red roof. But in the picture in my head, having a house I could call home was just as important as having a best friend. I was so happy I felt like skipping, but instead I just smiled to myself and kicked my feet through the pile of leaves.

Lucy stopped at her garden gate. She stayed in one of a row of identical brick houses that lined the main road. She'd lived there her entire life; something I could only imagine. My parents and I had been in Edinburgh for just over a year, which was a couple of months longer than we'd lived anywhere else.

Lucy pulled a square package, wrapped in silver tissue paper, out of her bag. "Happy birthday, Edda," she said, handing it to me.

"Thanks," I said, smiling so wide my cheeks hurt.

"Aren't you going to open it?" she asked.

I didn't need to be asked twice. I tore off the paper. Inside was a small blank book with a picture of a lion on the cover. The painting looked familiar.

"I got it at the National Gallery," Lucy said. "It's from that painting you liked so much when we went there with school."

"*Una and the Lion!*" I exclaimed, finally recognising it. "It's the best painting in the whole building." Not only did I wish I could paint that beautifully, I also wished I could have a lion for company like Una. Then I wouldn't be afraid of anything.

"Is it a good size?" Lucy asked. "I wanted to get

something small enough to fit in your pocket so you can do your art wherever you go."

I told her it was perfect, not wanting to admit I was too shy to even think about drawing in front of other people.

I gave Lucy a quick hug and continued on my way home, daydreaming about the presents waiting for me and the chocolate mousse cake I'd spied at the back of the fridge, even though Mum had sworn she wasn't making one this year.

I'd almost reached the top of Hillside Drive when a cloud passed in front of the sun and the street darkened. Some sound made me look behind. Huffing and puffing, Euan Morrison was pedalling up the road on an expensive new mountain bike. I had to hide. Euan's favourite hobby was picking on me, and no one was here to stop him. Luckily, he hadn't seen me yet. He was too busy watching his feet go round and round. I slipped behind a stubby rosebush and crouched down. Most of the time it stinks to be the smallest kid in class, but when you need to hide it can be useful.

Euan drew nearer. I held my breath. If he caught me skulking like this, he'd never let me live it down. He'd moved to Edinburgh last September just like I had. Kids had ignored him, just like they'd ignored me. We could have banded together, become friends even, but he decided the fast route to popularity was finding someone to make fun of: me.

I watched through a gap in the leaves as he rode past, still wearing his uniform. He stayed somewhere on the other side of school in a neighbourhood full of big fancy houses, so what was he doing here? At the crossroads, he turned up the hill, towards my house. I gulped. Did he know where I lived?

I told myself I was being silly. Euan was lazy. He could humiliate me all he wanted at school. He was probably just going mountain biking. An iron gate at the top of my street led to Corstorphine Hill Nature Reserve. Lots of kids like Euan, with more muscle than brains, spent their afternoons on bicycles, hurtling down the park's steep, winding paths at break-neck speeds – literally. I hoped Euan would fall, not so badly he'd be hurt, just enough to scare him.

I counted to fifty, then left my hiding spot and walked slowly to the crossroads feeling angry with Euan for invading my neighbourhood and spoiling my perfect afternoon. I looked up the empty street. The gate was swinging back and forth in the wind.

It was only when I turned into my yard and Henry, my neighbour's golden retriever, came bounding over to the fence, that I noticed the sun had come back out.

My house, a snug little bungalow, looked even smaller than it was because the trees in the park behind it grew so tall. All that separated my back garden from that park was a stone wall and a green wooden door. When we first moved in, Mum said the door reminded her of *The Secret Garden*, that it made all of Corstorphine Hill Nature Reserve feel like our own magic place.

Dad's a woodworker and he loves having the woods close by. He says it makes it easier to live in the city, having nature just the other side of the wall. We moved to Edinburgh when Mum got a job teaching botanical illustration – that's painting pictures of plants for scientists – at the Royal Botanic Garden.

The house was empty but the whine of a band saw and the comforting smell of sawdust told me Dad was in his shed in the back garden. I went into the living room to investigate my presents.

There was a big squishy parcel from Granny and Grandpa Ritchie in Canada: probably a jumper. Granny Ritchie always knits me jumpers and they're always at least two sizes too big. I only see her every few years and she never believes Mum when she sends my measurements – both my parents are normal sized. Nana Macdonald had sent something small in a hard box, jewellery maybe. She has very particular ideas about girls being ladylike.

The presents from my parents were more difficult to guess. They know how much I like to poke and prod my gifts, so they always disguise them, hiding them in extra-big boxes or using wads of bubble wrap to give them strange shapes. I'd asked for a set of professional oil pastels and an iPod. None of the packages looked right for either, but a couple were big enough to hide them inside. I'd have to wait until after dinner to find out.

I left my homework in my bag and went into my bedroom to get my sketchbook. The pictures I drew in it were just for me: things I found interesting, places I visited, stuff from my dreams, portraits of friends and caricatures of people who bugged me. No one, not even my parents, was allowed to open it. When I wasn't using it, I kept it safely hidden under my mattress.

As I pulled it out of its hiding place, a small piece of paper fluttered to the floor: a leaflet for a contest at the National Gallery. Lucy had made me pick it up. The contest was called "Put Yourself in the Picture". To enter, you had to "interpret" one of the gallery's paintings by copying it and adding an image of yourself. The deadline was the first of October, which was only two weeks away, but I still hadn't gone back to the gallery. The idea of anybody seeing something I'd drawn was frightening enough; displaying a picture I'd made of myself was completely petrifying.

I folded up the leaflet and tucked it inside my sketchbook. I turned to a blank page and took out the box of broken, grotty pastels I'd had since I was six. Some of them were smudged so badly it was hard to tell what colour they were meant to be.

I closed my eyes and tried to remember the way everything had looked as I walked home. As soon as the image started to form in my head, I began to draw. I had no problem sketching Lucy and me, but when it came to adding the hill and houses I kept thinking about Euan being there and the picture went all wonky. The trees came out dark and menacing and the houses were crooked, not cosy at all. I pulled the page out, crumpled it up and started again. I'd just got the sun the way I wanted it when the front door banged open. I looked at the clock beside my bed. It was six thirty already!

"Sorry I'm late," called Mum. "Where is everybody? Aren't we picking up Lucy in ten minutes?"

"Coming," I said, shoving my sketchbook into its hiding place.

There was a knock on my bedroom door and Mum entered. "You're still in your school uniform!" she exclaimed. "And your hands are covered in pastel!" I looked down at them; they were a mess.

"Where's your father?" she asked. His band saw started whining again, so I didn't bother answering. "Hurry and get cleaned up," she said. "I'll pry your father out of his shed."

I wiped my hands quickly on a tissue and rummaged through my clothes until I found what I was looking for: a brightly coloured dress, because I'd picked a Mexican place for dinner; and red shoes with heels, because going to a restaurant for my birthday seemed like an adult thing to do.

"Oh, Mouse, you look so grown-up," said Mum, as I came into the hall. Edda the Mouse, that's me. My parents have been calling me that for as long as I can remember. It might have been cute when I was six, but I've hated the nickname for a while now. It's hard to be anything but small, quiet and timid when you hear "Mouse" more often than your real name. I'd kind of hoped they would stop doing it when I turned thirteen.

"Mum—" I began, but just at that moment Dad burst out of my parents' bedroom in his one, very out-dated suit, pleading for someone to sort out his tie. Mum got it knotted and herded us both out the door and into the car.

Dad slipped behind the steering wheel. He still had large flakes of sawdust in his hair. I looked down at the traces of pastel that were still on my hands and smiled.

*

I'd never tried proper Mexican food before, but the gooey cheese enchilada I ordered was delicious and I cleaned my plate – well, except for the fiery green hoops of sliced jalapeno pepper. After accidentally biting into one of those, I picked out the rest and piled them safely to the side.

After dinner, we dropped Lucy off at her house and Dad turned the car up Hillside Drive. I hugged my knees to my chest, feeling warm inside from dinner and the anticipation of presents.

Mum nattered on about work. Dad nodded every once in a while to show he was listening. We were out late. All that was left of the day was a faint blue glow in the sky behind the black hulk of the hill. As we turned onto our street, I sat up extra tall, waiting for the exact moment our house would appear out of the darkness.

Mr Campbell's house swung into view, windows glowing, but in the space before it, the space where our house should have been, all was shadowy blackness. For one crazy, awful second I thought our house was gone. Panic fluttered in my stomach, but then the headlights swept over its beige stone walls and curtained windows. I leaned back, feeling foolish for imagining a building could just disappear.

Dad pulled the car into the driveway. He and Mum got out. I lagged behind, unable to shake the feeling of uneasiness, like an itch that was everywhere and nowhere at the same time. The house was still here, but something was wrong; I knew it in the hollow of my stomach. This house was the first place we'd stayed in that really felt like home; if anything happened to it,

I didn't know what I'd do.

I opened the car door. I could hear Henry barking. Was it my imagination or did he sound anxious? I got out and looked over. He was at Mr Campbell's front window. He saw me. The barking stopped and was replaced by the thumping of his tail hitting the glass. He wasn't worried about anything. I was just being silly. If I wanted my parents to stop calling me Mouse, maybe it was time to stop acting like one.

"Edda, are you coming?" Mum called from the front door. "There's chocolate cake." The mention of chocolate chased away the last tingle of uneasiness. I skipped up the stairs and followed Mum inside.

"I thought you weren't baking a cake this year," I shouted, hanging up my jacket.

"It wouldn't be a birthday without your favourite cake," Mum said, poking her head out of the kitchen. "I was only teasing before."

"You shouldn't joke about chocolate," I said. She gave me a mischievous grin and vanished back into the kitchen.

A minute later she called, "Edda, can you please get Great-Granny Macdonald's plates out?"

I could hear someone rooting through drawers, probably trying to find the candles.

I turned the lights on in the living room. The china cabinet was empty.

"Where'd you put the plates?" I asked.

"What?" Mum shouted back.

As I stepped into the room, my foot kicked something. It rolled under the sofa. I bent down to see what it was:

a wadded-up ball of gold and purple wrapping paper. I looked over at the coffee table. Where the neat stack of presents had been, there was a mess of torn tissue paper, cut ribbons and ripped-up cardboard. The mammoth set of pastels I'd asked for had been dumped onto the floor, the magenta ground into the carpet by someone's shoe. Next to it sat an empty, watch-sized box with the crest of a Kirkcaldy jeweller on it.

My brain struggled to make sense of it.

"Mum, Dad," I said uncertainly. Panic danced in my stomach.

"Just a minute, honey," Mum called. "Nathan's finally found the candles. Why don't you put on the birthday CD?"

There was a gaping hole on the side table where the stereo should be. Someone had been in the house while we were gone. They might still be here now. My brain screamed "run" but my feet were glued to the floor. I opened my mouth to shout for help, but no sound came out.

"Okay, you can hit play now," said Dad, carrying a cake into the room, thirteen candles blazing on top.

"What's wrong, Mouse?" he asked, catching sight of my face.

My voice still wouldn't work. With a shaking hand, I pointed at the table, the cabinet, the place where the stereo should have been. Dad dumped the cake on the table and strode over to the phone, bellowing, "Helen, get in here, now!" as he picked up the receiver and dialled 999.

## 2. SLEEPING WITH THE LIGHTS ON

"They'll send a police officer as soon as possible, but since it's not an emergency it might take a while," said Dad, hanging up the phone.

"Not an emergency?" I said. "But someone broke into our house. They stole my presents." It felt like they'd also stolen the invisible warm bit that had made the house feel like home. I shivered.

"We'll buy you new presents," said Mum. I wondered if it was possible to buy back that warm, safe feeling too.

"What if they're still here?" I continued. My stomach churned as I imagined a man in a balaclava lurking in my bedroom, listening to us talk, waiting for his moment to leap out.

"I wouldn't worry, Mouse," Dad said gently. "They got what they wanted. They're long gone now."

"Let's wait outside anyway, just in case," I said, desperate to escape the house that still looked like ours, but felt like it belonged to strangers.

"Mouse..." Mum began. I bolted out the front door before she could finish her sentence.

I waited for my parents to follow, but the door remained shut. The night began to close in around me and I shuddered.

A door slammed. It sounded like the back door to our house. I felt sick. Was it a burglar running away? Was he creeping towards me around the side of the house?

Where were my parents? Weren't they worried about me out here all alone surrounded by robbers?

I had a sudden sickening thought. What if they had surprised the burglar and he'd knocked them unconscious before running out the back door? What if they were lying on the floor bleeding, needing my help?

Once I had the thought, I couldn't get it out of my head. I had to go back inside and make sure they were okay. I was thirteen now, it was time to stop being Edda the Mouse and start being someone else, someone braver.

Mustering all the courage I could find, I took a step towards the house. The handle on the front door rattled and began to turn. I froze. The door swung open and Mum emerged in her winter jacket, carrying my big warm coat in her arms. Relief swept over me, making my knees wobble.

"I thought you might want this," she said. She wrapped the coat around my shoulders and I snuggled gratefully into its warmth.

"Where's Dad?" I asked, my voice still shaky.

"He went to check the shed," she said. Her hand reached into her pocket. Seconds later it came back out, empty. I recognised that gesture. She'd made it a lot after she quit smoking. Watching her do it again, I knew she was upset too. The lump in my throat grew bigger.

"I should never have dragged us to the city," Mum said quietly, gazing at the house. "Maybe we should think about moving."

I thought about having to change schools again, about leaving Lucy behind. I thought about Henry. Who would take him for long walks if we left? I hated that our house had been broken into, but I didn't want to move away.

The sound of a car winding up Hillside Drive broke the silence. A police car appeared at the crossroads, turned up our street, and came to a halt in front of our house. A light came on inside it. I could see the police officer leafing through a notebook. The longer he sat reading, the more Mum stiffened and bristled beside me. Finally, he got out and came over to us, trampling straight through Mum's flower border without even noticing.

"Is this the B and E?" he asked her.

"If you're asking if we're the ones who called about a burglary, then the answer is yes," said Mum coldly.

The police officer looked like he'd be more comfortable in a uniform one size bigger. He brought a hand up to his mouth, stifling a yawn. I could actually hear Mum's jaw clench.

"Sorry," he said, "long day." Mum stared at him as though she'd have more sympathy for a midge.

"Well, show me the damage," he said.

Mum pursed her lips but said nothing, just turned and walked to the front door, the policeman in tow.

I lingered behind, which was when I heard the squeaking and saw the boy on the old-fashioned bicycle for the very first time.

When Mum, Dad and I were all gathered in the living room, the policeman asked us loads of questions. Did we usually leave the house on Tuesday nights? Who knew we were going out? Had there been work done to the house? My parents answered, no, nobody, and no.

"I wouldn't worry too much," he said, smiling jovially. "Looks like a professional job. If they didn't have inside information, they must have had your place staked out."

It sounded like a lot to worry about: someone watching our house. The thought made my skin crawl.

"Do you know how they got in?" the policeman asked. "Any broken windows? Broken doors?"

"I checked the back door. It was unlocked," said Dad.

"Was it locked when you left?" asked the policeman.

"Yes... at least I think so, but I keep a spare key under the mat," said Dad, looking guiltily at Mum. "The key's gone," he added.

"Then it wasn't really a *break* and enter," said the policeman, chortling at his own joke. Mum looked at him as if he were a midge she wanted to squash. "It's better if they get in easily," the policeman continued, "that way you don't have to repair anything. Replacing a window or a door can be costly. Better get the locks changed though. These professionals know that once you get the insurance money, you'll replace what they took. They could come back."

My stomach flip-flopped. What if they came back one afternoon when I was here by myself?

"Speaking of insurance claims..." The policeman handed Mum and Dad a stack of papers, explaining they had to write down each missing item, its brand, age, the room it had been taken from and what it had cost. One copy was for the police, one for the insurance company and one theirs to keep. He said not to bother rushing to fill them in, since they had a backlog of forms to deal with anyway. Mum's jaw ticked.

"Well, that's it for me," he said cheerfully. "I'll not keep you from your celebrations any longer." He waved a hand in the direction of the cake and the mess of torn wrapping paper.

"Aren't you going to look around?" Mum asked.

"Nah," he replied. "I see this sort of thing all the time."

"Well then, thank you for all your help," Mum said through clenched teeth.

"My pleasure," he replied, oblivious to the sarcasm in her voice.

While my parents walked him to the door – "to make sure he leaves," Mum muttered – I started tidying up. I gathered the shreds of wrapping paper and dumped them in the recycling bin. Then I collected all the pastels. Some were broken, while others had been smudged together. The only pastel that still looked brand new was the gold one, which was useless. When would I ever need to use a gold-coloured pastel?

I succeeded at holding my tears back until I saw the fuzzy pink jumper Granny Ritchie had sent me lying on the floor. Someone with muddy shoes had stepped on it and torn the shoulder. As I picked it up, the stitches started to unravel. The jumper was two sizes too big and I never wear pink, but watching it fall apart made my eyes fill up and overflow. I wiped my cheeks, folded up the jumper and laid it carefully on the table.

Mum came back in and grabbed one of the forms, announcing she was too wound up to go to bed just yet. I peeked over her shoulder as she noted the missing presents: an iPod and a Swiss watch.

Catching me looking, she tried to give me a smile, but it came out more like a grimace. "It's okay," she said. "We'll buy new ones."

I trailed after her and Dad as they went from room to room writing things down. They left my bedroom until last. I paused at the door, afraid of what I'd find on the other side.

*I will be brave*, I told myself. I gritted my teeth and followed them in.

The burglars had dumped my dresser drawers out onto the bed and my jewellery box gaped open. Necklaces and earrings were strewn across the desk. My stereo and even my crummy old clock radio were gone.

Mum flicked through my jewellery. "Her amber necklace is missing," she told Dad. He wrote it down.

That's when I noticed my mattress was hanging off the bed frame. Feeling like I might throw up, I walked slowly around to the far side of my bed. My sketchbook lay open on the carpet, the flyer for the contest ripped in two beside it. My eyes threatened to overflow again. Someone had come in here, put his hands under my mattress, pulled out my most private thoughts and looked at all the stuff I wanted to keep secret.

I felt just as exposed as I had on my first day at Hillside High School when Euan stole the doodle I'd made of me as a mouse and showed it to the whole class, crowing, "Eddie the Wee Mousie", and making a stupid face. I'd wanted to say something clever, but my mind went blank. The other kids started laughing and calling me Wee Mousie too. I'd wanted to crawl under my desk and hide, but I couldn't move.

Lucy had rescued me. She strode up to Euan, who's at least a foot taller, pulled the notebook out of his hands and gave it back to me. Since that day, Lucy and I have been friends and making fun of me has been Euan's favourite pastime.

I suddenly remembered that Euan had been in my neighbourhood just a few, short hours before the burglary. He knew it was my birthday, thanks to Mrs Doak. He might even have overheard Lucy and me making plans to go out for dinner. Maybe he hadn't been going mountain biking after all. Maybe he'd come up here to spy on my house.

I told myself I was being silly. Euan was certainly mean enough, but the police officer had said it looked like a professional burglary and there was no way Euan had the brains to pull off something like that.

Mum stayed and helped me clean up. While we folded clothes and untangled necklaces, she kept telling me I didn't have to sleep in my bedroom. She could get out the air mattress and put it on the floor by their bed.

I wanted to say yes. The idea of being alone in the dark in a room someone had broken into terrified me. But abandoning it felt too much like giving in to the burglars, so I said I was fine.

Mum stayed until I was safely tucked into bed. "Goodnight, Mouse," she said, kissing me on the forehead. For once I didn't mind the nickname; it made me feel safe and warm and sleepy. My eyelids sagged shut, but as soon as the door clicked closed behind her, they snapped back open again. The room was pitch black. Mum had turned off the lights on her way out. Heart pounding, I pulled the duvet up to my chin.

Had anybody checked under the bed? What if one of the burglars was hiding under there, waiting for me to go to sleep?

I lunged off the bed, and felt along the wall for the switch.

As soon as the light was back on, my fears dimmed, but I still needed to check that the room was empty.

I grabbed my hockey stick from the wardrobe and jumped back onto my bed. Holding it in front of me, I carefully leaned over and looked underneath. The only things lurking there were a couple of dust bunnies.

No one in the wardrobe, no one under the bed, and nowhere else large enough for someone to hide in. I leaned back onto my pillow with a sigh of relief, telling myself I was completely safe. I sat up straight again –
unless someone broke in through my window.

I left the light on. Clutching my hockey stick, I

crawled back under the duvet, determined to stay awake the whole night. But without the dark to fill my imagination, my mind began to settle and I started to feel sleepy. I tried to keep my eyelids open, but they grew heavier and heavier. As I drifted off to sleep, I heard the faint *squeak, squeak, squeak* of a bicycle wheel that needs greasing.

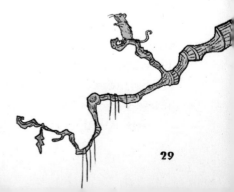

# 3. THE BOY ON THE BIKE

I woke, heart pounding. Something had banged outside my window. I was too scared to open my eyelids until I noticed I could see pink through them: daylight. The long night was over.

The noise began again: hammering. I groaned and rolled over to check the time. The spot where my clock had been was bare.

I felt awful, like I'd slept too long and not long enough all at the same time. My mouth was dry and raspy, and my jaw ached from grinding my teeth. I stumbled out of bed and rummaged through my dresser. Everything was in the wrong place but I finally found all the bits of clothing I needed for school: white blouse, not too wrinkled, navy skirt and jumper, and a pair of black tights. I got dressed, dragged a comb through my tangled hair and opened the curtains. Dad was at the back of the garden, nailing boards across the green wooden door.

I gulped. Had the burglars come in from the park?

I looked up at the trees that had been my friends and wondered why I'd never noticed how gnarled and twisted their branches were, or how they loomed over the back garden. As I imagined men dressed in black creeping through them towards our house, balaclavas pulled over their faces, the park that had been my playground seemed to shift in front of my eyes into a place that was unknown and dangerous. I shivered and drew the curtains, shutting out the view.

I could hear the familiar clink of dishes being unloaded from the dishwasher; Mum was still home. Instead of going to find her in the kitchen, I walked down the hall to the living room. The half-unwrapped presents were still piled on the coffee table, the chocolate cake beside them, thirteen puddles of wax on top of it. I'd forgotten about the candles. If I could blow them out now, I knew what I would wish for. I'd wish to feel safe again. It wasn't fair that someone had sneaked in and stolen my home from me. Tears – this time angry ones – gathered in the corners of my eyes. I balled my hands into fists and bit down hard on my lip, refusing to cry again.

Mum picked that exact moment to walk in. She put her arm around my shoulders and the tears started flowing out.

"Don't worry, Mouse, we'll go shopping, replace what they stole," she said, rubbing my back. I didn't think what they'd stolen could be replaced that easily.

Mum insisted on driving me to school. I tried to tell her I was fine, that I could walk the half-mile on my own as I'd done pretty much every day since we moved here, but Mum said she wanted to have a word with my teachers. My heart sank. I didn't want them to know. I didn't want them to smile sympathetically and treat me like I might break. I wanted to pretend nothing had happened.

I'd slept through most of the morning and by the time Mum got me to school it was lunchtime, so at least I didn't have the humiliation of being walked to class by my mother. She went off to the staff room and I went looking for Lucy in the playground.

As I passed the rows of chained-up bikes, something caught my eye. At the end of the nearest rack was an old-fashioned, upright, red and chrome bicycle, gleaming as if it had never been ridden. I was just reaching over to find out if its wheels squeaked when Lucy called my name.

"Where've you been?" she asked, jogging over. "Did your mum let you sleep in as an extra birthday present?"

For an awful moment I thought I was going to burst into tears right there in front of everybody.

"Oh," said Lucy, catching sight of my face. "What's wrong?"

I took a deep breath, pushed my tears deep down inside where they hardened into ice, and filled Lucy in on everything that had happened – right up to having to throw out my uneaten birthday cake because chocolate mousse needs to be refrigerated. Lucy's big brown eyes got bigger and bigger as I told my story.

"You must have been so scared," she said.

"It wasn't too bad," I lied. "Houses get broken into all the time." Wasn't that what the police officer had said?

"You are so brave," said Lucy. "If it was me I don't think I could have slept at all. I would've huddled in my parents' room all night with the lights on."

I shrugged. It felt good being this strong, brave Edda — even if it was only a story.

Just then, Mum came outside, spotted us and hurried over. She laid her hands on my shoulders and stared down at me, her forehead wrinkled with concern. I knew she was only showing me that she loved me, but I had to fight the urge to wriggle out from under her hands. How could I be brave Edda when she was so worried about me?

"Mrs Doak says you don't have to stay at school today if you don't want to. She's getting a list of assignments from your other teachers. You can come home with me."

"No," I said immediately. Going back to that house was the last thing I wanted to do.

"All right," she said to me. She turned to Lucy. "Take good care of my little Mouse, won't you? She's feeling fragile today." My cheeks burned with embarrassment, but Lucy nodded seriously.

Right on cue, as soon as Mum pulled away from the kerb, Euan moved in.

"Widdle Eddie's mummy had to bring her to school cos she's not big enough to walk on her own," he said, swaggering over.

I pretended to be interested in the scuffmarks on my shoes, but I could feel my face turning red.

"What'd she call you?" asked Euan.

"Nothing," I mumbled, scared he'd heard her.

"'Nothing' would be a good nickname for you, but that wasn't it," he said, smirking. "You're such a timid Wee Mousie even your mum forgets your real name."

He had heard her! I wished I really was a mouse, then I could scurry off and hide.

"Go away, Euan," said Lucy. "No one cares what you've got to say."

"Look after my Wee Mousie, won't you?" said Euan in a falsetto voice that sounded nothing like my mother's. He sauntered off, sniggering.

"I don't know why you let him bother you," said Lucy, which was easy for her to say. Euan left her alone.

The bell rang and I trailed glumly into school with all the other kids. I could tell Lucy any story I wanted, but it wouldn't change who I was: timid, meek little Edda who couldn't even stand up to a lame bully like Euan.

Someone bumped my elbow. A voice I'd recognise anywhere whispered in my ear, "Is widdle Eddie afraid of the dark?"

Heart racing, I whirled around but Euan was gone.

He knew! Euan knew what had happened. What if the police were wrong and it was personal? I knew Euan couldn't have done it on his own, but he might have had help. He was always bragging about his tough older brother.

The crowd of students pressed in on me. I felt dizzy and breathless. I had to escape the hallway or I would suffocate. I turned to flee but my way was blocked by a tall gangly boy.

"Excuse me," I mumbled, pushing past him. It wasn't until I'd reached the safety of the girls' toilets and splashed cold water on my face that I realised he was the boy I'd seen last night.

By the time I was sure I wasn't going to faint, or worse, I was late, but Mrs Doak just smiled at me sympathetically and waved me to my desk. Thankfully, Euan wasn't in my history class, which took up the whole afternoon. If I got lucky, I wouldn't have to see him again today.

As I took my seat behind Lucy, I noticed the gawky black-haired boy sitting in the back corner of the room. I was so surprised, my jaw actually dropped open.

"Is he new?" I whispered to Lucy, nodding my head towards the corner.

Lucy glanced over. "Yeah," she said. "He started this morning."

"What's his name?" I asked. It was strange to think I wasn't the newest kid in the class any more. That had never happened to me before.

"It's..." Lucy frowned. "That's odd. I don't remember."

We both swivelled round to look at him. He ignored us. Again, there was something not quite right about him. He was wearing the school uniform, but his trousers had a line down the front, a crease, like they'd been ironed that morning; and the collar of his shirt was too pointy, like it dated from before he was born. By daylight, I could see his round glasses were made of thick, heavy plastic. He had a book open in front of him, but it clearly wasn't *Scotland Through the Ages*, which is what we were supposed to be reading. His book had an ancient, cracked leather cover and gold-trimmed pages. He scribbled something in it with a fountain pen.

Mrs Doak was the kind of teacher who always chose students who weren't paying attention to answer her questions. I couldn't concentrate at all, but thanks to my mother, she left me alone. I kept waiting for her to ask the new boy something, so I'd hear his name, but she ignored him too.

About a minute before the end of class, he put away his book, folded his hands on his desk and sat looking out the window. I watched him out of the corner of my eye, only half listening to Mrs Doak explaining our homework assignment. As soon as the bell rang, the boy was the first out the door. I shoved my books into my bag and rushed after him, but he was already halfway down the hall. Just my luck, Euan appeared at the other end, heading my way.

I couldn't face Euan, not after what he'd said about the dark. I was about to turn around and slink out the gym door when the strange boy collided with him. Euan's books went flying. He turned towards the boy, red-faced and scowling, fists raised. The boy's back was to me, so I couldn't see what he did, and they were too far away for me to hear their conversation, but all of a sudden Euan's face drained of colour and his hands dropped to his sides. To my complete astonishment, he stepped out of the way so the boy could pass.

How had he done it? How had he made Euan back down? Euan had a nose for misfits, and clearly the boy did not fit in, but Euan had let him go, untouched. It made no sense.

Just at that moment, Lucy came out of the classroom. "In a hurry to get home?" she asked.

"Yeah," I lied.

She caught sight of Euan. "You want to go out the gym door?" she asked.

I nodded.

# 4. THE GREAT MICHAEL SCOT

By the time I got outside, the boy and his shiny red bicycle were gone, but Mum had reappeared. She waved to me from the gate, our car illegally parked in the spot reserved for the bus.

I sighed. Mum's fussing always made me feel even younger and more helpless than I normally did. "You want a ride?" I asked Lucy, not wanting to face Mum on my own.

"No, that's fine..." she began, but I gave her the big-eyed puppy-dog look I'd learned from Henry and she laughed. "All right, as long as your mum doesn't mind."

"You could even hang out with me, visit a crime scene," I said hopefully.

"Oh," she said, looking more like a sad dog than I ever would because she meant it. "I'd love to come over, but I've got fiddle lessons in an hour. I'm really sorry." Lucy is the only person I know who actually wrings her hands – rubbing one over the other – when she feels bad about something.

"No worries," I said, surprised how disappointed I felt.

Mum let Lucy out at her house and then, instead of turning the car onto Hillside Drive, she went in the other direction, towards the south end of the city.

"Fancy some tea and cake?" she asked.

I thought about the wet thud my uneaten birthday cake had made when it hit the bottom of the rubbish bin. "Not really," I said.

"Well, I do," said Mum in a fake, bright voice, driving towards Morningside Road.

Normally I love going to Loopy Lorna's. It's this crazy little teashop with hand-knitted animal tea cosies and huge slices of cakes and traybakes, but today I just ordered some "honey bunny" tea and let it cool, untouched, on the table in front of me.

"I don't know what your father was thinking buying a house next to such a wild place," Mum said, pushing morsels of uneaten apricot slice around her plate with her fork.

"You like wild places," I reminded her.

"Yes, but they're too dangerous in the city. You never know who might be hiding in them. I don't want you spending any time in the nature reserve by yourself any more."

I sighed and looked at the lion tea cosy, hoping it would give me some sympathy. It stared back at me with its googly eyes. I could guess what was coming next.

"I'm going to start asking around," Mum said, "find a good neighbourhood with a better school. Morningside is nice. Wouldn't it be great to be able to walk to this place?" she asked.

"Are you going to finish your cake?" I asked. "Because I've got homework to do."

Mum looked down at her plate like she'd only just remembered it was there.

"I guess I'm done," she said, pushing it away. "Let's go home."

I sat at my desk, my homework laid out neatly in front of me, but I couldn't get started on it. My gaze kept straying to the place where my clock radio used to be, to the hockey stick by my bed, to the spot on the carpet where I'd found my sketchbook. I didn't want to move houses, I wanted to stay here, where I could go to Hillside High School with Lucy, walk Henry on Corstorphine Hill and carry on as if nothing had changed. I was angry with my mother for giving up so easily, but I knew what she was feeling because I was feeling it too: the house didn't feel like ours any more.

I abandoned my homework, grabbed my sketchbook and pastels and went out the back, hoping my special treatment at school would last another day. I dragged a musty old folding chair into the middle of the lawn, sat down and started to sketch the garden, the wall, the boarded-up door and the trees behind it.

Drawing usually absorbed me completely. Everything else would melt away while I worked at getting a picture just right. Trouble was, this picture wouldn't come out the way I wanted. The wall turned out uneven; the rocks jumbled together as if they were about to fall down. The boards Dad had nailed over the door looked like toothpicks that a baby could snap in two.

The trees looked gnarled and sinister. Even the friendly old beech that grew less than a metre from the back of our wall came out looking sinister in my picture. And the bit of lawn I'd drawn was uneven and splotchy, as if creatures lurked underneath, churning up the soil.

I'd hoped by drawing I could make the garden and park my own again, but fear had crept into the picture.

I scribbled across the page with my black pastel. I hated being afraid in my own garden. I glared at the door in the wall. If I could just peek out and make sure nothing skulked behind it, then maybe the forest would go back to being its old friendly self. But the door was nailed shut.

I'd had enough of the back garden, so I folded up the chair and dragged it through the gate to the front yard. I sat down and tried to draw my house, but I couldn't shut out my worries at all. I thought about what Euan had whispered in my ear. I imagined him breaking in, opening my presents, dumping my clothes out on the bed and leafing through my drawings. My hand shook as I moved it across the page and this drawing turned out even worse than the last. The colours were bright and ghastly, the lines wonky. The bungalow looked empty and crooked, like a haunted house.

As I stared dejectedly at the horrible picture I'd drawn, I heard the same *squeak, squeak, squeak* I'd heard the night before. I looked up in time to see the new boy cycling by.

"Wait," I shouted, dropping my sketchbook on the chair and running to the hedge.

The boy stopped in front of Mr Campbell's house

and turned to stare at me. Henry barked loudly at the window. The boy glanced at him and the barking stopped.

"You're the new boy, right?" I said.

He stared at me with his unblinking eyes for so long I thought he wasn't going to answer. "Maybe," he said finally.

If he was trying to intimidate me, it wasn't going to work. I was no longer the newest kid in the class.

"I'm Edda Macdonald," I said, doing what I thought a braver Edda might do: holding out my hand.

He got off his bike, propped it against Mr Campbell's fence and came towards me.

"Michael Scot," he said, giving me a strange, shallow bow. "With one T. As in *the* Michael Scot," he added.

I shrugged, letting my unshaken hand fall to my side. It seemed a perfectly ordinary name.

"Don't you pay any attention in history class?" he asked, which annoyed me. He'd been the one reading something that obviously wasn't his textbook.

I shrugged again, beginning to wonder if no one talked to him because he was a stuck-up twit with no social skills.

"Michael Scot," he repeated, yet again. "Only the greatest figure in all of Scottish history: renowned mathematician, astronomer to one of the greatest emperors Europe has ever known, *alchemist*." He said the last word with reverence.

"Like a magician?" I asked, quite sure we'd never studied anyone like that and doubtful that an emperor's magician would have a name as boring as Michael Scot.

"No," he said with an indignant snort. "Magicians are charlatans. They use trickery to prey on the gullible. An alchemist follows a higher calling. He seeks knowledge and wisdom and the answers to great mysteries, such as how to turn lead into gold."

Turning lead into gold sounded like magic to me, but if I said so, he'd probably blether on for another ten minutes. "I'm named after a Viking," I said, to change the subject. "I know it doesn't go with being the smallest in the class," I added to prevent him from pointing it out.

He just stared at me. The boy had the emotional range of a toaster. I was beginning to regret calling him over.

The silence between us stretched on. "Are you going to the park?" I asked finally, just to end it.

He nodded, the corners of his mouth tugging up into a brief smirk. "Would you like to come along?" he asked.

"I can't," I said quickly, startled by his invitation. "I'm not allowed." Not exactly true.

"Ah," said Michael, as if he understood everything. "Your parents won't let you into the park. Probably wise of them, given how small you are and the fact that you're a female."

"It's not that," I said hotly. "I used to go by myself all the time. It's just that we had a burglary, that's why the police car was here, and Dad thinks they came through the back garden, so now Mum doesn't want me to go to the park on my own any more."

He stared at me for a second longer than was comfortable, blinked and said, "If you came with me, you wouldn't be alone. I think you're just too frightened to come."

I recognised a dare when I heard one. Edda the Mouse would have ignored it, but if I wanted to take back my home and my park, I'd have to be brave. Besides, maybe I could go with him down the trail that ran along behind my house. Then I'd be able to see for myself that nothing was hiding behind the wall.

# 5. THE TOWER

"Who is he?" asked Mum, gesturing out the window at Michael, who was waiting by the hedge with his bike. "You've never mentioned him before." She seemed to be looking for any excuse to stop me from going.

"Yes I have," I said. "He's the one who biked by last night. He's new in my class and he's kind of awkward, so no one's taken the time to get to know him." None of which was a lie. "I thought I should show him around, since I've had so much practice being the new kid."

I was mad at her. When I'd come in to tell her I was going to the park with Michael, I'd found her on the sofa, with housing ads spread across the coffee table in front of her. I think she could tell I was mad too, because she folded up the newspaper and slipped it guiltily under her mug of tea. She agreed I could go, as long as I took her mobile and returned in an hour for dinner.

We walked up the road towards the gate, Michael pushing his once again silent bike.

"How come it only squeaks some of the time?" I asked, pointing at his bike.

"It never squeaks," he said, unblinking. "I keep it in perfect condition."

"Right." Who was I to contradict the Great Michael Scot?

He pushed the iron gate open. It groaned. "I suppose that didn't make a sound either," I said under my breath.

"Pardon?" said Michael.

"Nothing."

Michael pushed his bike through the gate and then held it open for me. I hesitated. My hands felt cold and clammy.

"If you've changed your mind—" Michael began.

"I haven't," I said, scurrying through the gate before I lost all my nerve.

Once I was through, I felt a little better. The same huge chestnut tree stood next to the path as always, like a friendly sentry. My breathing slowed and my heartbeat calmed.

"This is your journey," said Michael. "What do you want to do?" I was glad he was letting me choose, even though he said it in such a pompous way.

"I want to see the woods behind my house," I said, "to make sure there's nothing there."

"You're not going to find nothing," said Michael.

"Why not?" I asked, my stomach knotting. Did he know something I didn't?

"The universe is full of things. Even the air is made up of gases and saturated with dust particles and minute organisms."

"Yeah, I know that," I said, relieved that Michael was just being annoying again. "I meant nothing suspicious."

"You should always say exactly what you mean," he said, looking solemn. "Otherwise you could end up with something you don't want."

"Thanks," I said sarcastically. "I'll try to remember that."

"It may be possible to find nothing suspicious," he said. "But it will be difficult. We'll have to make sure that everything we come across is beyond reproach. I have some tools at my disposal, but we'll need to make a short detour to fetch them."

I checked the clock on my mum's mobile. "We don't have time to go to your house," I said, though I was curious about the kind of place Michael stayed in. "I've got to be home in less than an hour."

"Not to worry," said Michael. "I keep my tools close by."

He hurried along the main path. I followed behind at a trot, my short legs taking two steps for each one of his. Thinking about his house got me wondering about his parents and where he came from. His accent was Scottish, but I couldn't tell from which part exactly. I mustered up the courage to ask him.

He seemed surprised at the question, stopping to think about it. "If you mean where was I born, then in the Borders," he said, "Oakwood Tower, just outside of Peebles."

"We stayed in the Borders for a summer," I said. Mum had worked at Harestanes Woods. "No one there talked like you do."

"Well they wouldn't, would they," he said. "I've lived abroad most of my life." My question answered, he resumed his quick march along the path.

A place with the name Oakwood Tower sounded rather grand, but judging by his clothes, his old bike, and the fact that he was at our school instead of one of the private ones, his parents couldn't be all that rich. Maybe he was from a wealthy family but his father did something terrible, was disinherited, and they had to flee to Europe in the middle of the night...

"Edda," said Michael sharply, calling me out of my daydream. He'd left the main path and was heading up to the tall square stone tower that stands at the crest of the hill. I'd seen it hundreds of times, it's hard to miss, but I'd never bothered going right up to it before. Michael leaned his bike against the wall and started digging around in his satchel. I read the stone plaque above the thick, rusty old iron door:

CORSTORPHINE
HILL
TOWER

SIR WALTER SCOTT 1771–1832
ERECTED IN 1871 BY WM MACFIE OF CLERMISTON
PRESENTED IN 1932 TO THE CITY
BY W.G. WALKER C.A. F.S.A. SCOT.

Michael pulled a large metal key out of his bag and slipped it into the lock. To my amazement it turned. The heavy door swung open on its enormous hinges.

His family was rich and from the Borders. He had a key to this tower. It was all starting to make sense. "You're related to that famous writer from the eighteenth century, Sir Walter Scott!" I exclaimed, pointing to the plaque.

Michael inclined his head and smiled a small tight-lipped smile that didn't make him look any friendlier, but at least showed he had emotions. "Sir Walter Scott did indeed claim a distant relationship," he said. "It comes in handy from time to time."

He pushed his bicycle into the tower. I rolled my eyes. The boy certainly was full of himself.

"Are we really allowed in?" I called after him.

"Of course," Michael said, appearing in the doorway. "Why else would I have the key?"

I wouldn't put it past Michael to have stolen the key but I stepped through the doorway anyway. The tower was hollow inside. A spiral staircase made of iron took up most of the space, stretching upwards between whitewashed walls. At regular intervals, slits in the walls let in a small amount of daylight. I was itching to climb those stairs and see the view from the top.

Michael shut the door, locked it, and ran his fingers over its painted surface. "A good solid door," he said. "It was taken from the old Tolbooth Prison. Virtually impenetrable."

I wished we'd had a door like that in our garden

wall; then maybe the burglars wouldn't have been able to get in.

"Why such a thick door?" I asked, looking around. "It's not like there's anything to steal." All the tower contained was Michael's bicycle, a rusting metal chair and a box full of damp, wrinkled pamphlets.

Michael smiled thinly. "There's a magnificent view from the battlements. Why don't you head up?"

I didn't need to be asked twice.

I counted 99 steps, then another door. As I stepped onto the square roof high above the sea of trees, with Edinburgh and the countryside laid out at my feet, I felt like a Viking queen surveying her territory. In that instant, I decided I would do whatever I had to do to make Corstorphine Hill feel like home again.

I turned around slowly, taking in the view. Just a hundred metres away a skeletal radio tower stretched into the sky. Beyond it to the west I could see the airport, then the famous Forth Rail Bridge and the hills by Stirling, blue with distance, where we'd stayed one winter when I was three. I could even pick out the tiny smudge of the Wallace Monument. Turning northwards I could see tankers chugging up the Firth of Forth and the coastline of the Kingdom of Fife on the other side. Circling around to the east, there were the twin smokestacks of Prestonpans and farther still, the triangle of Berwick Law. To the south stood the dark brooding Pentland Hills and invisible beyond them, the Borders, where I had lived for a summer and where Michael had been born.

There was so much to see and so much I wanted to draw. I wondered if Michael would let me return with my sketchbook and pastels. I imagined him watching over my shoulder, breathing down my neck, telling me what I was doing wrong and going on about some exhibition he'd had in Paris as a toddler. I decided I'd rather not ask.

Then I remembered the gift Lucy had given me. I took the little book and a stub of pencil out of my pocket. I could draw without Michael ever knowing about it, but I had to hurry. The hour Mum had given me was ticking away.

I made a quick sketch of the Edinburgh skyline and reluctantly put the book back in my pocket. Only then did I think to look for my house. It was hidden behind the trees, but I thought I could see the edge of our neighbour's grey slate roof. If I was right, the house was closer than I'd thought. Michael and I could save time by cutting through the woods, instead of returning by the paths.

I left the roof, shut the door behind me, and started down the stairs. I was halfway down when that same feeling of uneasiness I'd had last night hit me. The tower was too still.

I raced down the remaining stairs. Michael was gone.

I tried the door. Locked. I tried to thump on it, but my puny fist hardly made any noise. My heart pounding, I grabbed the handle and shook it. What did I really know about Michael Scot? Nothing. Now he'd locked me up and left me here, where no one would think to look for me.

I remembered Mum's mobile. I took it out of my

pocket, sinking to the floor with relief as I dialled home. Nothing happened. I looked at the screen. No signal. The roof – I could get a signal from there.

As I stood up, I noticed Michael's bicycle. He never went anywhere without it. I doubted he'd leave it in here if he meant to hold me prisoner. I went around the box of pamphlets to get a closer look and nearly tripped over an open trapdoor. A set of stone stairs circled downwards, disappearing into the dark. Maybe Michael hadn't left after all.

"Michael," I shouted, cupping my hands around my mouth. "Are you down there?"

I heard a muffled sound. What if he'd fallen and was lying at the bottom of the stairs, unable to move?

"Are you all right?" I called.

Nothing.

"Okay," I told myself, "I'm going to be brave, strong Edda. Michael may be in trouble. I need to go down the dark, dingy staircase to find him."

My feet didn't want to cooperate. If only I'd brought a torch. I looked down at the phone in my hand and tapped one of the keys. The screen lit up. There was just enough light to show me each step as I descended into the ground.

After seven steps I could no longer see the trapdoor above, but the stairwell wasn't quite pitch black. I rubbed my eyes. In fact there seemed to be light coming from down below. As I descended, the light got brighter. I could see two steps ahead, now three. I put the mobile back in my pocket and hurried down the rest of the stairs, emerging into a small cluttered room.

I stared around in amazement. The room was the same width as the tower but circular. In the centre stood a thick wooden table, its roughly carved edges worn by use. An old hurricane lantern, like the one Granny Ritchie always brought camping, sat hissing on the table, lighting up the rows of shelves that lined the walls from the floor to the ceiling, which was six metres or more above. Jumbled together on the shelves were ancient books with cracked leather bindings, mangy stuffed animals and moulting birds, wooden boxes labelled with strange symbols, and hundreds of jars containing brightly coloured liquids, glittering powders, dried herbs, small shiny spheres that might have been fish eggs, ball bearings or rats' eyeballs, dried-up wizened chickens' feet, emerald beetle carcasses, tiny brass gears, sticks of charcoal and other things too bizarre to recognise.

Michael grinned down at me from his perch halfway up a wooden ladder that was attached to the shelves by a brass rail. I realised my mouth was hanging open and snapped it shut.

"As I mentioned, the so-called family relationship has its uses," he said, gesturing regally around the room.

I had to agree. It was the most fantastic place I'd ever been in.

"Put these on the table," he said, handing down two jars, one containing sparkling purple powder, the other dull grey. They were both coated with a thick layer of dust.

"Hey, if you're new here why does your stuff have dust on it?" I asked.

"I never said I was new," he said, coming down the ladder.

"Well, you're the newest in our class," I said. "And I think I would remember if I'd seen you around."

"Not necessarily," he said, turning his back on me and swivelling the ladder around to the other side of the room. He climbed back up it. I put the jars down on the table next to a big book. It looked like the one he'd been reading in class. It had an old leather cover and I could see now that it had the words *The Book of Might* written on it in gold. Curious, I opened it up.

"Don't touch that," shouted Michael. His words echoed around the room. Startled, I let go of the cover. It closed with a bang.

"That's private," he said more quietly.

"Sorry," I said, remembering how I felt when I discovered thieves had looked through my most private thoughts. "The burglars went through my sketchbook," I said. "I found it lying on the floor."

"Your sketchbook?" asked Michael, looking puzzled.

"It's where I put all my thoughts, all the important things that happen to me. I sketch them," I said shyly.

"Like any committed artist would," he said, nodding approvingly.

I looked at him with surprise. Had the Great Michael Scot just called me an artist?

"Cretins, like the thugs who invaded your home, don't understand that acts of great creativity require a certain amount of solitude and privacy."

"Right," I said. Maybe Michael and I had more in common than I'd thought.

He came down the ladder one-handed. In his other hand was a battered old jar full of a thick, bluish liquid. Suspended in the liquid was a fat bullfrog.

"I thought Benedict might come in handy," he said, setting the jar down on the table. "Frogs are expert at identifying insects," he continued, as if that explained everything.

"Even when they're dead?" I asked.

He ignored my question. I went back to thinking Michael was more than a little mad and that we really didn't have anything in common after all.

Michael lifted a carved wooden box off a shelf and placed it on the table. I watched as he removed the lid, expecting it to contain something fabulous or weird or just plain disgusting. Instead, he reached in and pulled out a couple of wadded-up plastic carrier bags from the local supermarket. He shook them out and put the jars of powder and the frog into them.

"When you said tools I thought you meant binoculars, a magnifying glass, things like that," I said.

"I've got those too," said Michael, moving the ladder yet again. "Somewhere."

I lit up the mobile to check the time. I had to be home in half an hour. "We need to leave now," I said.

"You go on ahead. I'll follow in a few minutes," he said.

I hesitated, shifting my weight from foot to foot, my palms sweaty again.

"I thought you were in a big rush," he said.

"But my mum said—"

"If you're too frightened to go alone, you'll just

have to wait," he said, cutting me off. It was another dare. The boy was infuriating! How could I have ever believed he'd be any help at all?

I turned my back on him and marched up the stairs. It was only when I got to the top that I remembered the door was locked.

"Michael, open the door," I shouted, my voice echoing off the walls.

"The key is hanging from the handlebars," he called up. Sure enough, there it was. Somehow I'd missed it earlier.

I unlocked the door, returned the key to the handlebars and left, swearing I'd never ask Michael for help again.

# 6. ALONE IN THE WOODS

What looked like a simple shortcut from the top of the tower turned into a maze on the ground. Normally I'm a fan of brambles – I love snacking on their juicy berries – but I'd only been walking for a minute or so when my way was blocked by a thicket too tangled and thorny to go through. By the time I'd gone all the way round, I wasn't sure which direction I'd been going in the first place. I looked at my watch and groaned. Mum expected me home in less than half an hour; I didn't have time to wander about in circles.

The tower stood on the highest part of the hill, which meant everything else was downhill, including the wall behind my house. I picked the steepest route I could find and started walking, but soon the ground began to level out. After a few more steps there was no more slope to follow. I came to another bramble patch and stopped.

I wished I'd waited for Michael. Sure, he was full of himself – how big does your ego have to be to call your journal *The Book of Might?* – and more than a little weird, but he was also smart and fearless. He'd know what to do.

Clouds had moved in. It was only just past five thirty, but daylight was leaking away. The park was beginning to seem unfamiliar and spooky again. A gust blew through the treetops, making the leaves mutter angrily to each other. I looked around for a landmark, but all I could see were trees. Somehow I'd got lost in a park that had once felt to me like part of my own back garden.

I remembered Mum's mobile and pulled it out of my pocket. No signal. That was strange; there was a huge radio tower somewhere behind me. But it was probably just as well I couldn't call. If I told Mum I'd disobeyed her, gone off on my own, and got lost, she'd never let me out of the house again. I sighed. I'd have to find my own way home.

*Once upon a time there was a little girl called Mouse who got lost in the woods*, I thought to myself. It sounded like the beginning of a fairy tale – a scary one with sorcerers and monsters. I forced myself to take a slow, deep breath and think what strong, resourceful Edda the Brave would do. She might use shadows to find her way, if the sun had been out. I wondered if Michael had a compass in his tower den. My parents always brought one when we went hill walking. Why hadn't I thought to do that?

"Michael's not here," I said to myself. "Lucy's not here. Your parents aren't here. You're on your own, so think." I looked around. "Line up the trees!" I exclaimed, more loudly than I meant to. Why didn't

I think of it before? I didn't have a compass, but that didn't matter. The park wasn't that big. All I had to do was walk in a straight line until I got to one of the roads that surrounded it. Then it would be easy to get home.

My parents taught me when you're out in the wild and you want to walk in a straight line, you find three things that line up in front of each other. I looked across the bramble patch and found three young beech trees that lined up on the far side. Keeping my eye on them, I walked around the thicket until they lined up again. I went to the first one, stopped and picked another further along that lined up behind the remaining two.

I'd been striding happily from tree to tree for about five minutes, feeling pretty pleased with myself, feeling like Edda the Unexpectedly Resourceful, when I heard a noise. It sounded like footsteps on dried leaves. I froze. Who else would be out here, away from the paths, at twilight?

A burglar?

Panic stirring in my stomach, I started walking again, faster than before. The footsteps behind me sped up too. I began to run, so did the person following me. I plunged through the undergrowth, no longer bothering to line up trees, just trying to get away from the burglar, but the faster I went, the closer the footsteps seemed to get.

The person following me shouted, but I couldn't hear what he said and I wasn't going to stop to find out. My breath coming in great rasping gulps, I ran as fast as I could. Branches whipped across my face. I kept stumbling on roots and loose rocks, but somehow

I stayed on my feet. I pelted past a clump of birch saplings. The ground beneath my front foot gave way. A dark hole opened up in front of me. I flung myself backwards, landing on my back in the birches. I lay between their slim white trunks, staring at the patch of gloomy sky above me, struggling to catch my breath, listening with mounting dread as the footsteps drew closer.

Michael's face swam into view. "Why didn't you stop?" he asked. "I tried to warn you."

Relief flooded me. It had been Michael all along, not a burglar.

"Why were you following me?" I croaked. It's hard to speak when the air's been knocked out of you. "You scared me half to death."

"You frightened yourself," he said irritably, as if he was the one who'd nearly fallen down a hole. "Has anyone ever told you your imagination is overactive? I said I'd catch up."

Grabbing the trunk of the nearest tree, I hauled myself unsteadily to my feet. Now that I knew where to look, I could see the hole easily enough. Long tufts of grass had grown over the edges, hiding them from view, but the hole itself was about a metre and a half across. I spotted a couple of rusted fence posts and a bit of rotten wooden railing. Someone had fenced it off a long time ago and then forgotten about it.

Corstorphine Hill was dotted with old wells like this one. They were supposed to be blocked off to prevent accidents. I picked up a pebble and tossed it into the hole. It bounced three times and was still. It sounded like the well was at least as deep as Michael's tower room. If I'd fallen down it, I could have been killed. I clamped my lip between my teeth to stop it from trembling. All I wanted to do was crawl into my bed and pull the duvet over my head. I looked at my watch and groaned. It was six o'clock and I had no idea where I was. On top of everything else, I was going to be late. I turned my back on Michael and began retracing my steps.

"Where are you going?" he asked.

"Home," I said.

"But we're almost at the wall," he said.

I stopped and glared at him. "I think I'd remember if there was a great gaping hole behind my house."

"We're not behind your house," he said. "We're downhill from there."

It would be quicker and safer to follow the path that ran along the wall than try to find my way through the woods.

"Fine," I said with a sigh. "Lead the way."

Michael had told the truth; in just a couple of minutes the treetops began to thin and the wall came into view.

We followed the trail up the hill in silence. We hadn't gone far, when the huge beech tree behind my house came into view. Michael stopped at the tree, took off his satchel and pulled out the jar with the pickled frog. I walked right past him and kept on going.

"What are you doing?" Michael called after me.

"Going home," I said. "I'm already late."

"Oh," he said, sounding disappointed, "I thought you wanted to look for nothing."

I stopped, turned and faced him. "I did, but we wasted too much time going to your stupid tower so you could get your dumb frog and all your other useless things."

"You also spent quite a bit of time wandering around the woods," he said mildly.

I was too angry to think of anything else to say, so I turned and started up the trail again.

"It will take you at least ten minutes to go that way," he called after me.

I wondered what he wanted me to do instead – fly?

"In case you haven't noticed, I don't have wings," I said, stopping again.

"You could climb over the wall and be home in a matter of moments."

I looked at the wall. It didn't seem so high. Michael was tall. With a boost from him I could probably manage it. Then I could sneak around the house and come in the front door, pretending I'd just come down the road.

"Okay," I said, walking back to the big beech tree. "Give me a leg-up."

Michael's lip actually curled. Despite talking like a grown-up, he obviously still thought girls had germs. Unbelievable.

"You'll have to do it yourself," he said. "I've got to let Benedict out for his evening constitutional."

"Fine," I said, feeling hurt even though I knew it was nothing personal. The boy didn't know the first thing about getting along with people.

The wall was old and many of the sandstone blocks

had begun to dissolve, leaving cracks big enough to stick fingers into, maybe even toes. I got two hands and one foot on the wall, but every time I tried to pull my second foot up, my fingers lost their grip and I came tumbling down. Michael deposited his frog in the grass by the green door, where it sat glistening wetly. He came back to watch my attempts at climbing.

"You know, helping people is a good way to make friends," I said, after I tried again and failed.

"You're doing it all wrong," he said.

"Is that your idea of helping?" I asked, annoyed.

"If you applied some simple principles of physics and made your best effort..."

"I'm trying as hard as I can," I said, showing him my broken fingernails. "And I think the simple principle of gravity is the problem."

"Ah," he said, nodding, "but friction is your ally."

I glared at him, Mr Know-it-All.

"The tips of your fingers don't provide enough surface area to produce the friction you need to keep your weight on the wall," he said. "But if you put your back to it..." He stepped between the beech and the wall. Leaning against the wall, he placed first one foot, then the other on the tree trunk and began walking up it, wiggling his back up the wall as he went.

I was impressed.

Michael eased himself onto the top of the wall, brought his legs up underneath him so that he was crouching and then leapt, landing nimbly on his feet beside me. He grinned. I found myself grinning back.

He took off his glasses and wiped them on his

jumper. "I forgot how much fun being a child can be," he said.

It was a sad thing to say. I remembered hearing his bicycle last night as I was falling asleep. What kind of parents let their thirteen-year-old hang out in a mouldy old tower on his own at night? I didn't know anything about his home life. Maybe he didn't know how to make friends because no one had ever shown him how.

"That's a good trick," I said.

"I know," he said, putting his glasses back on. "Your turn."

I crouched, pressed my back into the rough stones, and walked my feet towards the trunk. It was difficult going and the rocks poked painfully into my back, but I managed to shimmy up the wall.

"That wasn't too hard," I said, feeling pleased with myself as I sat on top of the wall.

"And if someone like you can do it, then anyone can," said Michael.

"What are you trying to say?" I asked, angry that he was making me feel like a mouse again.

"I merely wanted to prove that nailing your garden door shut isn't going to prevent people from sneaking in," he said. The light was dim, but I thought he was smirking.

"Thanks," I said. "That's very helpful."

"Wait there," he said to me, turning to look at his frog. He walked over to the door, knelt down, and pulled something out of the grass.

"Look what Benedict found," he said, walking back towards me, holding out a dark piece of wool. I had to lean dangerously low to take it from him.

"It is possible that piece of wool was up to no good," he said.

The wool was the same colour as our school uniforms. "It's from your jumper," I said, irritated.

"No it's not," he said indignantly. "I keep my jumper in perfect condition."

"Well, none of mine are frayed," I said. I suddenly remembered that Euan had been wearing his uniform when he rode past me yesterday. Was this proof that he'd been lurking back here, that he'd gone through the door into my garden?

I looked up the path. He could easily have ridden his bicycle down it. I looked at the trees in front of me, full of dark shadows. Even now, someone might be hiding, watching me and I wouldn't know it.

"I just wish..." I began.

"Wish what?" asked Michael eagerly, a strange, greedy look on his face.

I wished that everything could be the way it had been before, but I wasn't going to say something that childish in front of him.

"Nothing," I said. I turned my back on it all, Michael included, took a deep breath and jumped into my back garden. I didn't land as neatly as Michael, but I managed to land on my feet.

Mum's mobile buzzed. I took it out. The signal was back and there was a text waiting for me, demanding to know where I was. Mum had sent it five minutes ago.

I sighed. Drawing hadn't taken the fear away and going to the woods had almost killed me. How was I ever going to get my feeling of home back?

# 7. A PRESENT FROM EUAN

Mum insisted on driving me to school again the next morning. I was too tired to argue. I'd left my light on, but still had trouble falling asleep. I'd woken up more tired than ever, snatches of dreams chasing each other around my head.

I'd dreamed I was running through the woods, my clothes catching on brambles, something big and scary following me. I came to a clearing. A frog sat in the middle of it, gleaming wetly in the moonlight. It croaked, trying to tell me something I couldn't understand. The monstrous thing chasing me crashed through the trees behind me and I fled to the wall, scrabbling to climb up it, my fingers getting raw and bloody as the noise drew closer and closer. At the last second, I pulled myself onto the top. When I looked down the other side, I saw Michael standing in my garden, smirking.

Mum was late getting me to school again, but Mr Sheldrick said nothing. I supposed Mrs Doak had told him about my problems.

Lucy whispered "Hi" as I took my seat. I whispered "Hi" back.

I glanced over at Michael. He was scribbling away in his *Book of Might*. The boy had an ego the size of an elephant, the manners of a pile of bricks, and he talked to dead frogs, but he also got away with doing whatever he wanted, and he wasn't scared of anything.

Once I realised that paying attention in class stopped me from thinking about other things, the morning passed quickly enough. By PE I'd almost forgotten to be scared, until Euan appeared in the hall in front of me.

"I hope you like your present," he said.

I felt the blood drain from my face and my knees got all wobbly. I pressed my hand against the bank of lockers so I wouldn't lose my balance.

"I'll be watching you," he said, laughed, and sauntered off.

"Idiot," said Lucy. "You should report him to the Head."

"His jumper," I said. "Was it frayed? Were any threads missing?"

"What are you talking about?" she asked.

As we walked to our lockers I showed her the thread I'd got from behind the wall. She assumed I'd found it on my own. I didn't correct her. Then I told her about Euan cycling up my street the day of the burglary, and what he whispered in my ear.

"What if it was him?" I asked. "What if it was Euan who broke into my house, on my birthday?"

"I don't know," said Lucy. "It sounds like the burglars did a good job. They only took valuable things and they hid their tracks. Do you really think Euan could manage something like that?"

"But what he just said — he must have meant my birthday, stealing my presents," I said.

"No," said Lucy, "I think he meant this." She pointed at my locker door. Wee Mousie was written across it in red marker, surrounded by mouse stickers with their heads ripped off. Stick-figure girls' faces had been drawn on instead. For some reason, he'd also stuck on an apple sticker. A couple of older girls pointed and tittered as they walked by.

I took a tissue out of my pocket and tried to wipe the marker off. It didn't even smudge. "Great," I said. "Now I'm going to get detention."

"No, you won't," said Lucy. "Who would believe you wrote that on your own locker? See what I mean? Euan isn't smart enough to be your burglar."

I unlocked my locker and took out my PE kit. What she said almost made sense.

"But what about the things he whispered?" I said, shuddering at the memory.

"It's just the same thing he always does — he's saying you're a baby because you're small. Little kids are afraid of the dark. That's all."

"Just because I'm little doesn't mean I'm afraid of the dark," I said. But I *was* afraid of the dark. That was the problem.

"I didn't mean size," said Lucy. "I'm just as small as you. I meant younger kids."

"Yeah, you are the same size as me," I said, tired of the conversation. "So why doesn't he pick on you?"

"Because I ignore him," she said. "You should too. He just does it for attention and you give it to him every time."

"So you're saying it's my fault," I said, slamming my locker door shut. Lucy was really starting to annoy me.

"No, I'm saying..." Lucy trailed off. "Like when you drew that picture and Euan grabbed—"

"Yeah, I remember," I said, cutting her off.

"Euan was being totally thick, making that weird rodent face," she said earnestly. "If you hadn't turned all red and tried to grab it back, he'd have been the one who looked like an idiot."

"So I looked like an idiot?" I said, staring at her in disbelief.

"No, I mean—"

I walked away from her as fast as I could. I'd had enough of Lucy for one day.

"Edda," she called after me as I hurried down the hall towards the changing room.

I ignored her.

Lucy was my best friend, but sometimes she just didn't understand. Maybe she was right, maybe Euan wanted attention, but I didn't. No one knew who I was before Euan showed them the stupid doodle, and I was okay with that. Now most of them still didn't know who Edda Macdonald was, but if you asked them to point out Eddie the Wee Mousie, all their fingers would go straight to me.

When I returned to my locker after PE, I found Mr Speck, the janitor, scrubbing at Euan's graffiti with some foul-smelling foam.

"You know who did this?" he asked.

I hesitated a heartbeat too long.

"Right," he said, "go to the main office and have a word with Mrs Brown."

I hadn't done anything wrong. I was the victim, so it was totally unfair that he was sending me to see the Head.

He must have seen the stricken look on my face because he said in a softer voice, "You've got to stand up to bullies or—"

I turned and left.

When the Head asked me who'd marked up my locker, I was better prepared. I lied right away, saying I had no idea. I knew if I told on Euan it would only make things worse.

Mrs Brown seemed to believe me. She changed the subject to the break-in, telling me that if there was anything she could do I should come and talk to her. But when I got up to leave, she launched into the same old lecture about standing up to bullies that everyone was giving me. I guess I wasn't as convincing as I thought.

Euan was lurking outside the office. I turned to see if Mrs Brown had spotted him, but she was talking to her secretary.

I walked past Euan, ignoring him, but he fell in step beside me.

"Did you tell her?" he asked.

I kept on ignoring him.

"If you say anything to anybody, I'll—"

I stopped and turned to face him. Edda the Brave looked up at him and said, "You'll do what, Euan?"

He paused, and for a moment I thought standing up

to him really was going to work, but then he smiled a smile that looked more like a snarl and Edda the Brave fled.

"You'll find out what happens to wee mousies who snitch," he said and he sauntered down the hall like he owned it.

I was shaky after my run-in with Euan. I just wanted to find Lucy – she always made me feel better – but my visit to the Headteacher's office made me late for lunch. When I got to the cafeteria, Lucy was sitting with Christine and Beth Barre and a couple of other girls. There was no room for me. I told myself that was fine, because until she apologised I wasn't speaking to her anyway, but I didn't feel like eating my sandwich any more. I went outside to look for Michael.

I found him sitting on a tree stump at the back of the playground, his long legs crossed awkwardly in front of him. Not surprisingly, he was reading a mouldy old book in some language I didn't recognise.

"So how did you do it?" I asked him.

"Do what?" he asked, looking up.

"Yesterday, in the hall, Euan was going to hit you but you did something and he left you alone. What did you do?"

"Euan?" he asked. "Oh, you mean the large, blond chap who decorated your locker?"

I didn't think decorated was the right word but I nodded.

"Simple," he said. "He's just a common bully and with bullies—"

"I know," I said. "All bullies are really just big chickens and if you stand up to them they will leave you alone."

"Precisely," said Michael, returning to his book.

"But I can't," I said miserably. "I just get too scared and all I can do is run away and hide. And it probably seems stupid, but now with the house broken into I feel like bullies are everywhere and there's nowhere safe to hide any more."

I hadn't meant to confess all this to Michael, but now that I'd started, I couldn't seem to stop. "I'm tired of being a timid, scared little mouse all the time," I said finally.

Michael snapped his book shut. "Is that what you wish for?" he asked, his intense brown eyes fixed on mine. "An end to your fear?"

"I suppose," I said. I wanted to look away, his gaze was making me uncomfortable, but I couldn't.

"That's not good enough," he said. "The first thing you need to do, if you want your wish to come true, is to say it as though you mean it." He opened his book and started reading again.

"Fine," I said, to the messy-haired top of the pompous twit's head. "I wish I wasn't afraid all the time."

"Good," he said, looking up.

"What's the second thing?" I asked.

"You have to say it in front of someone who can answer your wish." He smiled like he knew something funny but wasn't going to let me in on the joke.

"But who... Oh," I said, understanding finally. "That's you, is it?"

He nodded, still smiling.

"You think you're a fairy godmother or something?" I asked.

"Or something," he agreed.

I stared at him in disbelief. I couldn't wait any longer for Lucy to apologise. If I had to spend another lunchtime with Michael and his humongous ego I might start helping my mother look through housing ads.

"There's a final thing to keep in mind," said Michael.

"Yeah, what's that?" I asked.

"Be careful what you wish for."

I rolled my eyes.

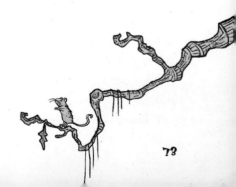

# 8. THE FIELD TRIP

Lucy came outside with Christine and Beth. They were giggling.

"So, what would make you feel less afraid?" Michael asked.

"I don't know," I said, distracted. "Maybe if I had something to protect me." I hated fighting with Lucy and I was worried she was having too much fun with the twins. What if she decided she liked them better?

"Are you sure that's what you want? Remember what I said about wishes."

"Oh, right," I said, tearing my gaze away from Lucy and the twins. "I wish to have protection for me and my house. Is that better?"

"It's clearer," said Michael. "But are you sure that's what you want?"

"Yes, I'm sure," I said. The boy took himself way too seriously. "Why? Is it too difficult for the Great Michael Scot to arrange?"

"Of course not," he said. "Though it would be easier if there was a proper physic garden nearby. Edinburgh used to have one of the finest in the world, but they built a train station on top of it." He sighed. "And they call that progress."

"My mum works at the Botanic Garden," I said. "They have a lot of plants there."

Michael snorted dismissively. "Their scientists wouldn't know a useful plant if they trampled on one. I bet there's not a single person there who has even an inkling of how to make a philosopher's stone."

"You read too much Harry Potter," I said.

"Harry who?"

I rolled my eyes. "Don't you have everything you need at the tower?" I asked, thinking about the rows and rows of jars I'd seen.

"It doesn't work that way," he said impatiently. "If you want to overcome your fear you have to collect the ingredients yourself. The Botanic Garden will have to do. Perhaps they keep more interesting plants away from the prying eyes of the public. Does your mother have one of those card devices that lets her into locked buildings?" he asked.

"What, the Great Michael Scot can't just throw some powder at the door and have it open on its own?" I said, my gaze wandering back to Lucy.

"Well, I could," he said, oblivious to my sarcasm. "But it would leave certain traces, certain odours and it's best if I keep my presence a secret."

*Yeah, the odour of pompous twit,* I thought to myself.

Christine said something. Lucy and Beth doubled over with laughter. I sighed.

"Mum's got an ID card, if that's what you mean," I said.

"Good," said Michael. "Bring it tomorrow. We'll go to the garden and collect what we need."

"Mum's still upset with me for getting home late last night," I said. "There's no way she'll let me go to the Botanic Garden after school."

"Would she let you go with the class?" he asked.

"Well, yeah," I said. "But how would we get the whole class to come with us?"

Michael just smiled. The bell rang and he strode off on his long, lanky legs. I didn't bother trying to catch up with him.

Lucy, however, seemed to be walking more slowly than usual. I hurried after her, hoping she was waiting for me, but as I drew closer she sped up again. I thought maybe she'd seen me and wanted to avoid me after all, so I hung back feeling more sad and lonely than I had in a very long time.

We had science after lunch and the teacher was late. I was about to lean forward and tell Lucy I was sorry – even though she was the one who should be apologising to me – just so we could be friends again, when Mrs Philpotts burst through the door carrying a messy stack of papers. Just as she got to the front of the class, she dropped them all. She knelt down and gathered them up.

"There's been some sort of mix-up," she said, getting to her feet, her broad face flushed. "I've just been informed that you're going on a class trip tomorrow. Here are the permission sheets," she said, handing out the papers. "Make sure you get them signed tonight and bring them in tomorrow. There will be no second chance. Yes, Edda?" she said, obviously surprised to see my hand in the air. I usually avoided talking in class.

"Um," I said, "you didn't tell us where we're going."

"Didn't I?" asked Mrs Philpotts. "You're going to the Royal Botanic Garden."

I spun around in my seat and stared at Michael, but he was too busy looking through the window with an enormous pair of binoculars to notice me. He'd got us a trip to the Botanic Garden, but how?

I barely listened to a word of the lesson. I was too busy wondering about Michael, who he was and how he'd changed the class schedule. I wished I'd paid closer attention to what he'd said outside. Had he told me what he needed to get at the Botanic Garden and why?

When the bell rang, he was the first out the door. I made sure to be second, but when I looked down the hall he was nowhere to be seen. I ran to the main door, but his shiny red bicycle was already gone from the bike rack.

I wandered back to my locker, wondering what I'd got myself into by agreeing to his help. I didn't think he was a fairy godfather, but it did seem like he could do things other kids couldn't. Was it this alchemy stuff he'd mentioned?

Lucy was at her locker, across the hall from mine. I took my coat out slowly, hoping she'd come over and ask if I'd walk home with her, but she kept her back to me and rushed off without even glancing in my direction.

The day had started out sunny but when I left school

it was dark and gloomy. The clouds were so low that the radio tower on Corstorphine Hill was invisible and the tops of the trees looked like they were fading away. Without the sun, all the shadows had disappeared. The world looked strangely flat and empty. I felt the same way inside: flat, hollow and alone.

The next morning, I waited until Mum went out to the shed to take Dad his coffee, then I crept down the hallway to the table where she kept her purse. The zipper protested loudly as I opened it. I stopped, holding my breath, but Mum was still outside. I rummaged around for her wallet, found it, and pulled out her ID card. I wrapped it in one of my woollen mittens to disguise its shape, stuffed it into my jacket pocket, put the purse back the way I'd found it and raced back to the kitchen. I'd just picked up my cereal spoon again, when Mum walked into the room.

As I was putting on my jacket, she came out into the hall. I froze, wondering if she somehow knew what I'd done.

"Why don't you drop by my office while you're there," she said. "It would be fun to have my daughter visit me at work."

"I can't," I said, leaning over to tie my shoes so she couldn't see the guilty look on my face. "It's a school field trip, they'll have activities for us to do."

I gave her a quick peck on the cheek and hurried out the door, telling myself that if Michael could actually do something to protect the house, it would be for my parents too. Besides, I was only going to borrow her card for the day.

It was a perfect day for a field trip as everyone, minus Euan, filed out of school and down to the bus. Euan had failed to bring a signed permission slip and was going to spend his day in the library doing homework, under the strict eye of Mr Bradbury the librarian. He'd looked forlorn sitting at his desk while the rest of us got our coats on, like a balloon that's lost its air. I would have felt sorry for him, if I wasn't so glad he wouldn't be around to bother me. I wondered if Michael had arranged it, just like he'd arranged the field trip.

I was bursting with questions, but Michael hadn't shown up yet. While all the other students got on board, I hung back, worrying that he was going to miss the bus. Mrs Philpotts waved me on. Reluctantly, I climbed the stairs. Lucy was already sitting with Christine. Feeling everyone's eyes on me, I took a seat by myself near the front. As soon as I sat down, Michael appeared. I was hoping he'd sit next to me so I could ask my questions, but he chose the seat directly behind the driver. Mrs Philpotts got on, ticked off all our names and sat down beside him.

I looked around. Lucy met my gaze and gave me a tentative smile. I smiled back. I was the only one sitting alone, but at least Lucy wasn't angry with me. It was a start. Maybe I'd have a chance to make up with her at the garden.

# 9. THE QUEST

The Botanic Garden's education officers met us at the bus and took us to the education centre, where we got to play with microscopes and learn how plants grow differently depending on where they're found. Then they gave us a sheet listing plants at the garden that were collected in different bioregions.

"When you find one of these plants, there will be a paper next to it with a letter on it. You need to collect all the letters to spell out the secret word. A prize goes to the first ones to return with the correct word. Pair up."

Lucy came hurrying towards me. "So do you—" she began, but Michael appeared at my side and glared at her. She shut her mouth and walked away.

"Wait," I called after her, but either she didn't hear me or was ignoring me.

"What did you do that for?" I said angrily. "I'd much rather work with Lucy than you."

"It's 'ecosystem,'" he said.

"What?"

"Now you know the word, let's get on with what we actually came here to do."

I'd been so excited that Lucy wanted to work with me, I'd completely forgotten the whole field trip was Michael's idea.

He pulled the form out of my hand and wrote E-C-O-S-Y-S-T-E-M in the nine boxes next to the plant names. "There, now can we get going?" he asked.

"Wait, you don't know that's right," I said. There are hundreds of other nine-letter words. Give it back."

He handed it back to me along with a handwritten list on a piece of parchment. "This is what we came here for," he said, tapping the list.

I read through it:

1 spine from a hedgehog cactus
1 petal from the world's largest water lily
2 grams of frond from one of the tallest palm trees
1 spider's web woven on an African violet
2 drops of mucilage from a Venus flytrap

"Mucilage, isn't that snot?" I asked. "You want me to collect plant snot?"

"You're confusing mucilage with mucous," said Michael. "Mucous is what comes out of people's noses. Mucilage refers to the gelatinous secretions of plants."

*Gelatinous secretions* sounded like plant snot to me, but there were bigger problems with Michael's whole plan than their ick factor. "I don't know about this," I said. "You heard the education officer; we're not allowed to take anything unless it's already on the ground."

"No one is going to miss a single cactus spine or a

single frond," he said. "Besides, we'll be doing the garden a favour. Plants need to be used to be appreciated, not just gawped at. Otherwise they lead half-lives, trapped in their plant zoo." My doubt must have shown on my face. "Look, I'm sure they'd give us what we need if we told them what it was for," he continued, "but they'd have to go through committee meetings, bureaucracy. It would take weeks, months even. Do you want to wait that long?" he asked.

"And what is it for?" I asked, reluctantly following Michael outside.

"It's to help you get rid of your fears," he said.

"Yeah, I know that, but what is it for exactly? What are we going to make with these things?"

"If you manage to get all the items, I'll tell you," he said, giving me an infuriatingly condescending smile. "If you fail, it won't matter."

"But—"

"Do you want my help?" he asked.

"Yes, but—"

"Then you have to do exactly what I say."

I came to the Botanic Garden with Mum a lot, so I knew my way around. In fact, I knew exactly where to find the first three things on Michael's list, which I thought was a good start. The lily and the cactus were kept in space-age looking glasshouses across from the education centre. They were open to the public, so I headed there first. Michael followed silently behind, watching me. I wondered if he was going to grade me on my questing abilities.

We passed through the door of the cactus house and came to a cluster of gigantic *Aloes*, which spilled out over the concrete walkway. I ignored them, heading for the other end of the building where most of the *Echinopsis* cacti grow. The gardeners had planted them far back from the path because, like their namesake the hedge-hog, they are covered in hundreds of needle-sharp spines. Looking nervously around to make sure no one was watching, I stepped up onto the loose sandy soil and made my way round a couple of large granite boulders to a tall, straight cactus that stood about one metre high. I could imagine that a fence made out of these would keep burglars out. I wondered if Michael had some magic way of growing them from just one spine.

I hesitated. I had a vague memory about something from the Americas shooting its prickly bits at people. Was it a cactus or a porcupine or neither?

The windows of the glasshouse whirred above me, opening automatically to let in fresh air.

"We don't have all day," said Michael. "This is one of the easy ones. Go on, it won't bite."

I waved my hand in front of the plant. The spines stayed where they were. I reached out to pluck one off, but they were so crowded together that I ended up getting pricked.

"Ow," I said, a drop of blood beading on the back of my hand.

"Excellent," said Michael. "It drew blood, means it's potent."

I glared at him and pulled off the spine.

"Next," said Michael.

*

We passed from the dry air of the cactus house into the heavy wetness of the rainforest house. As we walked through it, I could hear the steady dripping of water from the tangle of leaves above our heads. We went through another door, coming out at the end of a raised walkway, which took us across the temperate glasshouse at treetop height. At the far side was one more door, and behind it a huge pond, home to the magical water lily, *Victoria amazonica.*

The pond was covered in enormous leathery leaves that turned up at the edges like giant tea trays. Standing next to them made everyone – not just me – look small. I had a fantastic thought: maybe Michael knew a spell that would make me bigger. If I was bigger, I could be Edda the Brave instead of Edda the Mouse.

After Mum first took me to see the lily, I'd drawn a picture of it in my sketchbook. Only now that I thought about it, I'd had to copy a photograph of the flower because it only blooms at night; it's pollinated by beetles not bees. Just like I remembered, there was no flower. My heart sank. Was I going to fail my quest so quickly?

"Oh dear," said Michael smugly, "we'll have to come back after dark." So he'd known all along. Maybe he didn't even want me to succeed.

"We can't," I said. "The garden closes in the evening. Do we have to get exactly what it says on the list?"

"Of course," said Michael. "It won't work otherwise."

I scanned the pond. There were a few greenish-brown prickly buds, about the size of tennis balls, poking out of the water and something that looked like a big fleshy pink fist half submerged in it. Could that be an old flower? I tried to remember what was supposed to happen after it was pollinated.

"All it says on your list is petal. It doesn't say 'fresh' or anything, right?"

"Well, it doesn't say so but it probably should be—"

"There's something out there," I pointed. "It looks like it could be a flower. I'm going to go find out."

Before Michael could try and talk me out of it, I went over to the edge of the pond and leaned on the nearest lily pad. It bent under my weight, sending rings of ripples across the surface of the murky brown water, but it didn't sink. It might actually hold me up.

"If I crawl across this leaf," I said to Michael, "I should be able to reach it." I just hoped I was small enough for this to work.

"You know," said Michael, smirking, "in the backwaters of the Amazon, where this plant grows wild, there are leeches that specialise in going up people's noses to suck their blood."

I jumped back from the water. *I will be Edda the Brave*, I told myself as I approached the edge of the pond again.

"How tall are you?" asked Michael.

"Why?" I asked, suspicious.

"Oh, nothing," he said. "I was just wondering if the water would be over your head, in case you fell in."

"I know what you're trying to do," I said.

"Really?" asked Michael. "What's that?"

"You're trying to scare me," I said.

"Is it working?" he asked.

"Yeah," I said, my heart thudding noisily in my chest. "But that's not going to stop me. Go keep a lookout at the door, make sure no one comes in." I was fairly certain the garden rangers would frown on someone climbing on their plants.

Trying hard not to think about blood-sucking leeches or dirty water closing over my head, I placed both hands on the thick, rubbery lily pad. Slowly, cautiously, I drew one knee up onto it. The lily pad suddenly tipped over and I scrambled hastily back to dry land.

"Lie on your stomach," called Michael. "It will distribute your weight more evenly."

My heart pounding more loudly than ever, I slowly lowered my body onto the lily pad. To my surprise, it stayed afloat. I slithered forward. The plant rocked a little, but the sensation was pleasant, like being on a waterbed. I inched across the huge leaf until the tips of my fingers could touch the fleshy pink object. It was the flower, all curled up on itself. I wiggled a little further forward. The lily pad started to tip into the water. I grabbed at the flower, pulling off a petal, and scooted back as fast as I could.

"I did it," I said, holding the thick petal up for Michael to see as I scrambled to standing. I misjudged. My right foot sank ankle-deep into the pond. "Yuck," I said, stepping back onto the path with a squelch.

Just at that moment, Lucy and Christine walked in. Lucy looked straight at my soaked trainer but she didn't say anything. Christine whispered something in Lucy's ear, span around and walked back out again. Lucy made a note on the sheet of paper she was carrying, looked me in the eye and pointed up. A piece of paper with the letter "M" was hanging above the pond.

"Thanks," I mouthed, hastily covering Michael's list with the scavenger-hunt paper. Lucy smiled and left.

I looked at the paper. Sure enough, the water lily was number nine. Michael might be right after all.

I checked my watch and smiled. There was still half an hour left and Lucy, being as clever as she was, had already found the last plant. I sighed. I missed being friends with her.

The elegant Victorian palm house was only a short distance away, so I led Michael there next. There were no real walls to it, just tall columns made out of beige sandstone with enormous arched windows in between. The glass roof rose above it in two curving layers, like a cake, doubling its height. The tallest of the palm trees inside grew so high that it was pressed against the very top of the roof. Another piece of paper was taped next to it, this time with a "Y". I checked the scavenger hunt. The palm was plant number five.

"Looks like you were right about the secret word," I said to Michael.

"Of course I was," he said, inspecting the ground around the base of the tree. "They've cleaned up well. The only way of getting a frond will be for you to climb the tree." He beamed gleefully.

Besides the complete madness of shimmying up a twenty-metre tall tree, it was standing right in front of a ranger station and the ranger was already watching us curiously. I doubted even Michael would get away with climbing it in front of everybody. It was a good thing I didn't have to.

"It's not the only way," I said. "Follow me."

There are advantages to having a mother who works at the garden: I knew where to find the compost piles.

I led Michael out of the palm house and round the back. A path wound between it and a modern glasshouse, a chain with a small "No Entry" sign blocked it. Making sure we weren't being watched, I ducked under the chain and went around the corner. Knowing we were out of bounds made me even more nervous than when I'd crawled across a potentially leech-filled pond, but I hid my feelings from Michael as I pointed to the pile against the back wall. Two fresh fronds sat on top of it. I stuck a leaf in my rucksack. It had to weigh at least two grams.

"Three down, two to go," I said cheerfully.

Michael scowled.

## 10. GLASSHOUSES

I was about to flee back to the safety of the public area, when Michael reached into my coat pocket and pulled out the mitten with Mum's ID card in it.

"We still have the Venus flytrap and the African violets to find," he said, drawing out the ID and tossing the mitten back to me. "We'll most likely find them in one of those." He pointed to the complex of interconnected glasshouses where the scientists did their experiments. But before he could swipe the card through the lock, we heard voices.

"Quick," I whispered, "over here." I ran to a big brown wheelie bin and crouched down behind it. Michael followed at an annoyingly slow saunter.

"Come on," I hissed urgently.

He squatted next to me just as two men in white lab coats came around the corner.

"What was that?" asked one of them, looking in our direction.

"What was what?" asked the other man, unlocking the door.

"I thought I saw something go behind the bin."

I was sure my heart would give us away, it was pounding so loudly in my chest. What would happen if we got caught back here, where we weren't supposed to be?

"Probably just the cat that's been digging up the alpine plantings."

"Don't you think we should catch it then?" said the first man, beginning to walk towards us.

I pressed myself against the side of the bin.

"And do what?" asked the second man. "I'm sure the PR department would love it if employees started kidnapping local pets."

"I suppose," said the first man, turning back to his friend. They went inside. I let out the breath I'd been holding.

"Okay, that does it, we're absolutely not—" but before I could finish my thought, Michael stood up and left.

I groaned. He still had Mum's ID card. What if he ran off with it? I had no choice. I had to follow him.

My heart still pounding way too loudly in my chest, I slipped around the bin. Michael stood in front of the door. Staring straight at me, he swiped the card across the reader. The lock clicked. He opened the door and disappeared inside. I lunged forward, grabbing the handle just before it closed.

I entered the long corridor that ran across the front of the glasshouses. Michael was already halfway down it, striding along like he belonged. I scurried after him, feeling like a trespasser, which was exactly what I was.

He stopped in front of a door labelled "Carnivorous

plant study", and peered through the window, waiting for me to catch up. "This is the one," he said, swiping the card again.

As the door opened, swampy air and the smell of rotten eggs oozed out. I stepped past Michael, eager to get out of the exposed corridor, and found myself in a humid glasshouse filled with rows of shallow plastic tanks overflowing with stubby, muddy-green plants. A single large, dark terrarium stood vibrating in the corner. As I walked towards it, I could see the darkness inside was made up of a seething mass of flies crawling along the glass, searching for a way out.

"Awaiting the executioner," said Michael, coming up behind me. He flicked the glass with his fingernail. The flies took off, buzzing even more loudly as they circled round and round inside their glass cage.

"Let's just find a Venus flytrap and get out of here," I said. The place gave me the creeps. I couldn't imagine the kind of person who would want to spend his life feeding flies to plants, but I was sure I wanted to be as far away as possible when he returned.

Michael shrugged like he didn't care what we did and started walking down one of the rows of tanks. He stopped halfway along to coo lovingly at some red-veined, tubular pitcher plants. I stared at him with disgust. I didn't need to use my imagination; Michael was exactly the kind of person who would devote his life to insect-munching plants. He probably fed live flies to his dead frog.

I sighed. If I'd paired up with Lucy instead of going on Michael's stupid quest, we'd already be back in the education centre receiving our prize for finishing first.

At the back of the room I found three tanks crammed full with Venus flytraps, their green pods shut tight, bound together with long tooth-like tentacles.

I called Michael over.

"They've just been fed," he said. "You'll have to pry them open."

No wonder the flies were in a frenzy; they'd just seen their friends get eaten by plants.

I found a box of swabs by the sink, grabbed one and approached the carnivorous plants. Pictures of mangled, half-digested flies danced in my head. "Why do I have to do everything?" I asked with a shudder.

"Because it's the only way it will work," he said.

"The only way what will work?" I asked grumpily. I was getting tired of being bossed around for nothing. "Can't you just tell me what this is for?"

Michael actually tut-tutted me, like he was an adult and I was some little kid. "Not until you've proven you're worthiness," he said smugly.

What if Michael was having me on? What if he had no magic plan and he was just getting me to do these things for a laugh? I decided that wasn't possible, since Michael had no sense of humour.

"Look at that," said Michael in a breathless voice. I turned round to see what was so exciting.

One of the Venus flytraps had unclasped its tooth-tentacles and was slowly opening. To my relief it was empty of fly parts. I watched, fascinated. It was like some alien creature, half plant, half animal.

"Quick, the swab," he said.

I stuck the swab in the plant's mouth. The second it touched the little hairs inside, the pod started to close again. I tugged the swab out, hoping it had soaked up at least two drops worth of mucilage, and wrapped it in a plastic bag.

"Fabulous, aren't they?" said Michael, patting it fondly with his finger. I had to agree.

"Wait a moment," said Michael, frowning at me like I'd done something wrong. "You weren't frightened of it."

"Why would I be scared of a plant that's only big enough to eat flies?" I asked indignantly.

He stared at me unblinking for an uncomfortably long minute. "Well, at least fetching the last ingredient should give you a good scare. Spiders!"

I rolled my eyes at him. "I'm not afraid of spiders," I said.

"Some are venomous," Michael said. "They can kill with just one bite."

"There aren't any poisonous spiders in Scotland," I said.

"Ah, but the plants in here have been brought from all over the world," he said, his eyes sparkling happily. "A long-fanged spider might have stowed away on a plant sample and made a comfortable life for herself in a nice warm glasshouse."

"They put new plants in quarantine so things like that won't happen," I said. "If you'd paid attention you'd know that. Why do you want me to be scared anyway?" I asked.

"It's a quest," said Michael, as if that explained anything. "I noticed a sign saying 'Gesner house', that's

African violets, down at the end of the corridor," he said, changing the subject. "It's right next to the door to the building where the scientists have their offices. Doesn't your mother work in there too?"

I nodded, wondering what would happen if we got caught using her ID.

"All day, people go in and out through that door," Michael continued, staring greedily at my face. "Glasshouses being, well, glass, if anyone were to glance over, they'd see us in an instant." He snapped his fingers for emphasis.

The palms of my hands were getting sweaty. This time his attempt to scare me was working. "I'm not going with you," I said. "If you want the spider web, get it yourself." I checked my watch. We had to be back in ten minutes.

"But the quest—"

"You won't even tell me what it's for," I said. "For all I know, you could be winding me up."

"You're frightened," he said.

"Yes, I am. Are you happy now?"

He actually grinned at me.

"You're just a bully, you know that," I said, feeling really angry now. "You told me you'd help me get rid of my fears, but all you've done is try and make me feel worse."

"It's a golem," he said.

"What?" I asked. Had he gone completely mad?

"I know I shouldn't be telling you this, but you've done too well to give up now. We need the ingredients to make a golem."

"Gollum?" I said. "As in, 'My Precioussssss'?" I hissed, rubbing a pretend ring on my finger.

Michael stared at me unblinking for long enough to make me feel like I was a fly trapped behind glass. "No, I don't mean Tolkien," he said finally.

"So you do read normal books, ones that are written in English and come in paperback, not musty leather and gold," I said.

"Tolkien was a great man," said Michael, looking at me sternly. "He possessed an uncanny imagination for monsters. Most people's fears are completely banal, but Tolkien's had great scope."

"So if you don't mean Tolkien, what do you mean?" I asked.

"A golem, g-o-l-e-m, is a man made out of earth," he said. "A certain learned rabbi in Prague, whom I later befriended, worked out how to do it. He made one so big and fearsome, it held back a rioting mob, single-handedly saving an entire city quarter from destruction."

"A dirt man fighting a mob. I think I'd remember hearing about that," I said.

"It was before your time," he said.

"Of course it was," I said, "because it never happened. You can't bring mud to life, and definitely not with the mucilage of a Venus flytrap, a cactus spine and a bunch of other plant bits. Either you're playing a trick on me or you're mad."

"If you don't finish the quest, you'll never know whether I'm telling the truth, and everything you've done so far will be wasted," he said calmly.

The boy was infuriating, especially when he was right.

"Fine," I said. My anger with Michael had chased away my fear. "Let's go get a stupid web so we can make a stupid golem."

Michael smiled. "I knew you'd come round," he said smugly.

Palms now slick with nervous sweat, I followed Michael down the corridor and into the Gesner house. Two seconds after the glasshouse door closed, I heard the main door open. I dropped to my knees behind one of the tables of plants, my heart pounding. The sound of footsteps drew nearer. Michael kept walking around the room, poking at the plants. Hadn't he heard the door?

"Get down," I whispered, gesturing frantically at him.

He looked at me, his finger pressed to his lips, but he remained standing in full view. The footsteps paused. I held my breath. They started up again, fading away into the distance.

"Why didn't you hide?" I asked Michael, keeping my voice low. "You could have got us both in trouble."

"She wouldn't have seen me," he said.

"Are you crazy?" I said.

"People tend to overlook me, unless I want to be seen," said Michael, smiling in his favourite, self-satisfied way.

I thought about how he got away with reading his mouldy books in class and decided he was probably telling the truth. "Must be nice," I said, standing up and dusting off my knees. "Did you find any webs?"

"No," he said.

I'd just finished hunting through the plants on the nearest tables when the main door opened again. I hid. This time, there was more than one set of footsteps. Luckily, they walked past.

"Got one," said Michael, as I stood up.

I hurried over. A spider had woven a tunnel across the base of a large purple African violet. I took out my pen and started to wind the sticky strands around it. The spider poked her head out and stared at me reproachfully with her many eyes.

"Sorry," I whispered, "but I need your home to save mine."

She scuttled back under a leaf.

The main door opened a third time and I scrambled under the table. This time the footsteps stopped outside the glasshouse and the lock clicked open. To my relief, Michael joined me in hiding as someone wearing high heels entered.

I held my breath as the scientist bustled about, sure that at any moment she would spot me. Would my mother lose her job? We'd have to move then. Would I go to jail? I'd broken in here, just like the burglars had broken into my house. I felt sick to my stomach. This was all Michael's idea. It would be his fault when my mum lost her job, we had to move houses and I got sent to jail. I glared at him, but he was staring at the woman's feet.

I heard her turn the tap on at the sink. She was filling something. She turned the water off and came straight for the table we were hiding under. I scrunched up my eyes and waited for her to shout out in surprise. Instead, the phone rang. Her feet hesitated, turned and went back to the counter.

"Yes," she said. "I emailed that report to you." Another pause. "Do you need it now? I'm down in the greenhouse." She listened for a few more minutes then put the phone down without even saying goodbye.

I watched with grateful astonishment as the feet marched over to the door, the door clicked open, and the woman walked away.

Once the danger was gone, my quivering, shaking, sickening fear melted away and fury took its place. I was angry with Michael for nearly getting me in serious trouble, but I was mostly angry with myself for listening to him.

"Did that frighten you?" asked Michael with a fiendish grin.

I glared at him, crawled out from under the table and headed for the door without saying anything. I was afraid if I opened my mouth I'd start yelling at the top of my lungs.

"You can put that away now," Michael said, following behind me.

I looked at my hand; it was still clenched around my web-covered pen.

# 11. HEART OF CLAY

We escaped the glasshouses without meeting anyone, but we were late getting back and Mrs Philpotts was annoyed. Michael she ignored completely, but I got a lecture in front of the whole class about the virtues of punctuality.

Things only got worse after that. Michael and I were the last on the bus and everyone, including Lucy, was already sitting next to someone. Michael sat in the aisle seat behind the driver, making it obvious he didn't want to share with me, so I had to sit by myself again. The whole, long, humiliating drive back to school, I thought about how perfect everything had been before my house got broken into. I'd felt safe and secure, I'd had a best friend I could count on – now it was all slipping away. I couldn't do anything about the burglary, but I could make up with Lucy.

I was sitting at the front, so I was the first one off. I stood on the pavement, feeling awkward as the other kids streamed by. When Lucy came out the door I smiled at her hopefully and she smiled back. We both started talking at the same time.

"Look, I'm sorry—" I began.

"I didn't mean—" she said.

We looked at each other and laughed.

"Do you want to walk home with me?" I asked.

"Edda, I can't," she said, wringing her hands. "I've got to go to my aunt's. My little cousins have their music exams and I said I'd help."

Michael chose that moment to come striding over. He must have wanted to be noticed because Lucy definitely saw him. The two glared at each other until Lucy turned and walked away.

"What did she want?" he asked.

"Nothing," I replied.

"We still have a golem to make," he said. "Aren't you coming to the tower?"

"No," I said.

He just blinked at me owlishly.

"I have work to do at the library," I said. Before he could say anything else, I turned my back on him and marched into school.


I did have work to do – the history assignment I'd been avoiding all week – but when I got to the library I headed to the computers instead. I typed "golem" into Google. A surprising number of sites came up. At least Michael hadn't been making up the word. I looked through the list. Most talked about a legend from the Czech city of Prague. I read through a few of them.

A man named Rabbi Loew – who was a real person – made a golem in the 1500s to protect his people from a mob that wanted to kill them and burn down their houses just because they were Jewish. Imagining an angry crowd, spiky with pitchforks and torches, eager to hurt people just because they were different, made me feel sick. Luckily, the golem did its job and the rabbi and his people were saved. All the sites agreed about that. However, there were different stories about what happened to the golem afterwards.

Most sites said the golem served its master loyally for many years until the rabbi decided it had "outgrown its usefulness" and turned it back into lifeless clay, which seemed kind of mean. It hadn't really done anything wrong. As far as I could tell, when it came to monsters, golems were remarkably tame. I was beginning to think I might like to have one around, if Michael could actually bring mud to life.

I opened one more site. The golem in this story kept growing stronger and stronger until the rabbi couldn't control it any more. It turned on the people it had been created to protect and they had to hunt it down. Not such a friendly monster. Still, it was the only site with that version of the story, so maybe they'd got it wrong.

I'd had such success finding out about the golem, I decided to try "Michael Scot" too. There was nothing about an annoying thirteen-year-old who lived in Edinburgh and considered himself the supreme being of the universe, but there were a few mentions of the man he was supposedly named after.

The Michael Scot had been born in 1175 somewhere in Scotland. He'd spent a lot of time at school where his favourite subjects seemed to have been philosophy, languages, maths and astrology. He spent most of his life in Europe translating books with weird titles and, just like Michael said, he had worked for Emperor Frederick II. His death was a mystery. Despite being so famous, no one knew when, where or how he had died.

There were some strange stories about him too. Several sites said he could have any food he wanted brought instantly to his table just by clapping his hands. Another story said he'd got all his knowledge not from university, but from accidentally eating some old lady's snake stew.

As I walked home, I thought about all the things I'd read and I thought about Michael. He could do a lot of weird things, like get a field trip to happen when he wanted, and hide from people in plain view. He certainly knew things other kids didn't and read languages that were unrecognisable. He also had the most fabulous hideaway I'd ever seen, full of crazy stuff. He obviously hadn't been friends with Rabbi Loew, but what if the rabbi, or someone else who knew the secret, had written down how to make a golem in a book. Some of the books I'd seen in Michael's tower looked like they could be five hundred years old or more.

As I turned up the road towards my house, I could hear Henry barking frantically. Had something happened? I speeded up, my heart pounding in my chest. As I drew closer, I saw a red bicycle leaning against our hedge and I relaxed. Sure enough, Michael was sitting on the front steps, waiting for me.

"Ah," he said, standing up. "You've finished your little assignment?"

"Well, not—"

"Good," he said. "Shall we get on with the business of arranging some protection?"

"I'm not—"

"Time is flying by," he said, pointing at the cloudy sky.

He grabbed his bike and pushed it past me, heading towards the park gate. I hesitated, undecided. If – and this was a very iffy if – if Michael could show me how to make a golem, according to what I'd learned it would have to do what I told it to do. The golem would be my guard. I could sleep with the lights out again, knowing that no one would dare to break into our house.

"Wait," I yelled, running after him.

Michael laid a large marble bowl in the centre of the rough wooden table, next to the jar with Benedict in it. Then he climbed up the ladder and brought down a big box labelled "mineral clay, pure". He opened up his *Book of Might* and looked at me expectantly.

"Put the ingredients on the table," he said.

I took everything I'd got on my quest out of my bag: cactus spine, lily petal, palm leaf, swab with Venus flytrap mucilage, and the pen covered in cobweb.

Michael passed me a piece of marble shaped like a tiny club.

"To bring earth to life, all the other elements must be in balance," he said.

I thought about all the elements on the periodic table and wondered if Michael had them stashed away on his shelves.

"But there's over a hundred and I have to be home before my mum finishes work," I said.

"Not those elements," he said snidely. "The alchemical ones: fire, water, air and, of course, earth."

"Oh, right," I said sarcastically. "Those ones. Silly me."

"Fire first. Put the cactus spine in the mortar."

"The what?"

"The stone bowl," he said, pointing imperiously.

Scowling, I did as I was commanded.

"Now, grind it with the pestle seven times widdershins."

I had no idea what he meant by widdershins, but I guessed the pestle was the marble club. I started grinding.

"Stop," shouted Michael. "I said widdershins – anticlockwise."

"It would be easier if you just spoke English," I grumbled, but I reversed the direction of the pestle and counted seven times around.

"Good," said Michael, "now add the lily for water, and do the same thing."

By the time I'd finished seven more circles with the pestle, both the spine and the petal had been crushed to a paste.

"And the palm frond for air," he said.

When I was done, Michael measured two cups of powdered clay into the bowl.

"This isn't going to make a very big man," I said doubtfully, as I mixed the clay with the paste.

Michael snorted. "No, but it will make a good-sized heart."

I looked up, confused.

"What?" said Michael. "You thought we'd make the

golem in here? Have a great filthy beast lumbering around, breaking my jars, tromping on Benedict? Not likely."

"So where..." I began.

"We'll make the golem in the forest. That's where it belongs, tied to the earth of the hill. I just thought it would be easier to do the heart in here," said Michael. "It can be a little fiddly." He came over to inspect the contents of the mortar. The paste had mixed with the clay so that the bowl now appeared to contain a pile of greenish-grey breadcrumbs.

"Excellent," he said. He unscrewed the lid of Benedict's jar and poured some of his pickling liquid onto the heart-crumbs. "You'll have to knead it by hand to get the right consistency," he said.

"No way," I said, repulsed. "I'm not going to touch it now, with the stuff from your dead frog in it."

"There are gloves over there," Michael said, waving at one of the shelves.

Even with Michael's thick leather gloves on, I felt queasy as I put my hands into the bowl and started to press the clay crumbs into the dead-frog juice.

"Wipe this on it," said Michael, handing me the swab of mucilage. "The golem, like the Venus flytrap, hunts when it ought to be inert."

He unwound the spider's web and I had to work that into the mixture, which was beginning to form a ball. "To bind everything together," he said.

As soon as all five ingredients were in the clay, the slippery ball started to shape itself under my hands. It grew longer. One end thinned to a cone, while the other rounded itself out. I hardly had to do anything; it was as if the clay wanted to be a heart and was using my fingers to get into the right shape. When I was satisfied that the greenish-grey heart was perfect, I placed it back in the bowl, pleased with my work.

As I pulled off Michael's gloves, I noticed my watch. It was quarter to five. Mum would be home in fifteen minutes and she would be worried if I wasn't there.

Something at the edge of my vision moved. I looked at the heart. It was just a lump of clay, as still as ever. I began to turn away; the heart moved. I was certain this time. My own heart jumped. I stared into the bowl, unblinking, for a minute or more. The clay heart rocked a few millimetres from side to side. I gasped. Until that moment, I hadn't really believed Michael.

"It's learning to beat," he said, watching my face. "By tomorrow afternoon it will be ready to be placed in a body. You must meet me here after school and sculpt the golem itself."

I promised to come back and sprinted home along the path, feeling hopeful for the first time since the burglary.

## 12. THE LAST ELEMENT

Friday dragged by. All I could think about was the clay heart beating in the marble bowl and the golem I was going to sculpt out of dirt.

Lucy and I were friends again and Michael wasn't at school to mess it up, which would have been brilliant if I didn't have this great big huge secret. I wanted to tell Lucy everything, but didn't know how to do it without sounding completely mad.

During the last period of class, Mrs Philpotts droned on about sound waves. Without thinking, I started doodling on the blank piece of paper in front of me. I drew the mud man, making sort of a blueprint for how I would sculpt him out of dirt. I gave him big, strong legs and arms and a thick neck to support his huge head. His mouth was a vicious gash across his face. I was so absorbed in my drawing that I didn't notice class had finished until a shadow fell over my desk and someone snatched my picture away.

"Who's this, your boyfriend?" asked Euan nastily. He waved my picture in the air, but everyone else had already left.

"Give it back," said Edda the Brave.

"You want it so badly, go get it," said Euan, tossing it into the rubbish bin and spitting his gum out on top. I felt angry and helpless all at the same time. I clasped my hands together to stop them from shaking and tried to think of a come-back, but Edda the Brave had disappeared.

I must have looked as upset as I felt because Euan laughed in my face. I hung my head, fighting the urge to cry – which is when I noticed the edge of his navy jumper was unravelling. Before fear could freeze me entirely, I reached out and pulled the loose thread. It came away in my hand. Euan turned and sauntered away without even noticing. I shoved the thread into my pocket. Maybe Michael would have a way to tell if the wool we'd found by my garden door came from the same jumper as this one.

For the first time since my birthday, Lucy and I walked home together. Before I left her at her gate, she asked if she could come over tomorrow morning. I agreed immediately. As I continued up the hill, I decided I'd tell her everything in the morning. The golem would be real by then.

I planned to go home, change out of my school uniform and go to the tower, but when I got to the house, I saw the car in the driveway. Mum was home. My heart sank. All I'd thought about all day was creating the golem; now it seemed I'd have to wait. I didn't bother to ask if I could go to the park by myself. I already knew her answer.

I went to my room and lined the two threads up on my desk. They looked identical. I took my jumper off and lay the threads on top of it. Also identical. I sighed. I wasn't getting any nearer to proving Euan was involved. I tied a knot in the piece I'd stolen from him this afternoon, so I could tell them apart.

The doorbell rang.

"Mouse, your friend's here," Mum called. I winced at the nickname. I really should ask her to stop calling me that.

I tucked the threads into my pocket and went to the door. Michael stood in the hallway, awkward and out of place. I felt an unexpected flood of gratitude. He'd come to find me.

"Edda the Mouse," he said, smirking. "How apt." My gratitude faded.

"What do you want?" I asked, though I knew the answer.

"You promised to meet me," he said in a low voice.

"Mum wouldn't let me go on my own," I whispered.

"Well, you're not on your own now, are you?"

"Mum," I yelled, "can I go to the park with Michael?"

Mum appeared in the kitchen doorway, wearing her glasses. She was holding the housing section of the paper and a red marker. "If you take Henry with you," she said. "I saw Mr Campbell earlier and he was limping again. You know how he is about asking for help."

Michael, who was standing just out of Mum's view, shook his head vigorously.

"We'd love to," I said, eyeing the paper. I could see

red circles drawn around a couple of places. The sooner the golem was protecting our house the better.

Michael scowled at me, hanging back as I pressed Mr Campbell's doorbell. I could hear Henry barking in the background.

"Hiya, Edda," said Mr Campbell, coming to the door. "What can I do for you?"

I explained that we were going for a walk on Corstorphine Hill and wondered if we could take Henry with us. "For the company," I added, so he wouldn't think my mum had put us up to it.

"Please, get him out of the house," said Mr Campbell. "I don't know what's got into him, but he's been barking and whining and pacing the living-room floor for the last half hour. Henry. Come here lad," he shouted. But Henry, who usually came bounding to the door when he heard my voice, would only come as far as the living-room doorway.

Mr Campbell blinked, seeming to notice Michael for the first time.

"Have we met before?" Mr Campbell asked, peering at him. "You look like someone I knew when I was young."

"No I don't," said Michael stiffly.

A look of confusion crossed Mr Campbell's face. He squinted at Michael. "No, you don't," he said finally.

"You'll have to excuse me, sir, I'm needed elsewhere," said Michael. To me he whispered, "I'll meet you at the tower." Before I could say anything, he got on his bike and rode up the street, his wheels squeaking noisily.

As soon as Michael was gone, Henry came into the

hall. I crouched down so he could give me a sloppy kiss. Mr Campbell passed the leash to me, still muttering that he knew Michael from somewhere. I promised I'd have Henry back in an hour.

Henry pulled me all the way to the park gate, but when I tried to go up to the tower, he tugged in the opposite direction, down towards the meadow with the rabbits. I grabbed his leash with both my hands and yanked on it. He sat down.

"If you don't come with me, I have to take you home," I told him.

He must have understood because he got to his feet. He let me drag him up the path, but the closer we got to the tower, the more he lagged behind. When the tower finally came into view, he sat down again and refused to go any further.

"Come on," called Michael, waving from behind the tower. "You've got lots of work to do and not much time before Mummy wants you home."

"Coming. Maybe. Does one of your jars have dog treats in it?"

Michael ignored my question.

"What am I going to do with you?" I asked Henry. He looked at me mournfully with his big, liquid-brown eyes.

"I know," I said to him. "Michael's not my favourite person either, but he's okay really."

Henry whined.

"If you just come and sit and be a good boy while I make this man out of dirt, I promise I'll take you to chase rabbits when we're done."

His ears perked up at the word "rabbits". I tugged gently on his leash. Reluctantly he stood up and followed me, his tail clamped between his legs.

We found Michael in a small clearing in the woods, about a hundred metres beyond the tower. Benedict sat in his jar on a boulder behind him. Although the clearing was close to the paths, once I stepped into it, everything grew perfectly silent. A thick ring of bushes circled the edge, and there was an odd mist about the place. I could only see it if I looked at it sideways. If I stared at the mist directly, it melted away.

I tied Henry to a tree. He retreated into the undergrowth as far as his leash would let him.

"You're not much of a dog person, are you?" I said to Michael.

He grimaced. "They are animals," he said, "and like all animals, they are afraid of what they don't understand."

"Maybe, but I bet they'd like you better if you were nicer to them," I said. "Actually that works with people too. You might want to try it."

He gave me one of his unblinking glares and handed me the shovel.

"This clearing is two and a half metres long," he said. "A decent height for a golem. If you make it a metre wide, it should be able to defend you and your house from anything that comes along."

It would also be a lot of digging.

"I read about golems yesterday," I said. "Well, actually I read about one golem, in Prague, but it was just a fairy tale. Right?" I wanted Michael to convince me it could be done. "I mean the heart in the bowl looked like it was beating, but I still don't see how it can be possible to bring mud to life."

"What are you made of?" he asked.

"Flesh and blood," I said.

"But the atoms in your flesh and blood, where did they come from?"

"What I've eaten?"

"And what you've drunk and breathed," he said. "Every atom inside you was part of the air or the water or the soil once upon a time. All we're going to do is speed up the process."

"So you really know how to do it?"

"I told you, I studied abroad—"

"Yeah," I said, cutting him off, "you've mentioned it once or twice. So if I build a dirt man, you'll bring it to life and it will protect my house like a guard dog."

"No," said Michael, a look of pain crossing his face. "Not like a guard dog. The golem will be much more ferocious, and much more loyal. It won't let anything harm your property and while you are at home, it will protect you too. However, we are making it from the earth of Corstorphine Hill, so it can never leave the hill. It cannot help you at school. Do you understand?"

So not exactly a bodyguard, except when I was on the hill. "Do you mean the whole of Corstorphine Hill or just the nature reserve?" I asked.

"The nature reserve is a human fabrication," said Michael. "So long as it's touching the original soil and rocks of Corstorphine Hill, the golem can roam wherever it wants."

"Even back gardens?" I asked. Michael nodded. "But not roads?"

"No," he said. "The tarmac is made from gravel quarried elsewhere."

I'd still be on my own at school, but at least I could feel safe at home again. I used the shovel to draw an outline on the ground and then set to work. I dug soil from outside the line and packed it down on the inside. It felt good to work in the dirt, to dig and pat and create something from nothing just with my bare hands. Following my blueprint, I built up a thick heavy body and gave it two sturdy legs, two strong arms and a big bald head on a broad stubby neck. I cut a gash across his face for his mouth and poked two holes above it for eyes.

Michael brought the heart from the tower. It had dried to a silvery-grey colour, flecked with green, and was as hard as a stone. I dug a little hole in the creature's chest, and picked up the heart. I expected it to move again, like it had yesterday, but it stayed still and cold in my hand. I wondered if I'd imagined it beating, but I shook off my last remaining doubts, placed the heart inside the golem and packed dirt over the top of it.

"It's done," I said, standing up and brushing the damp earth off my knees.

"Not quite," said Michael, pulling his enormous *Book of Might* out of his satchel. "You need to carve these letters on its chest." He opened up the book and pointed to the middle of the page:

פתד

It didn't look like any language I knew.

"Write them exactly as they appear here," instructed Michael, passing me a long straight stick. "Use this. It's made of ash, which will give the word greater potency."

I wiped the creature's chest smooth and drew the first letter. I was about to carve the second one, when a thought popped into my head. "Will it, you know, be alive when I finish the word?" I asked. I wasn't sure I wanted to be this close to the creature when it woke up.

"Of course not," said Michael. "Creating life requires energy."

"You mean like electricity?" I said.

"Precisely," said Michael.

"So then what are the letters for?" I asked.

"You ask a lot of questions," said Michael. "Can't you just do as you're told?"

I put my stick down. "If you don't like my questions, you can do it yourself," I said.

Behind his glasses, Michael's dark eyes flashed with irritation. Through clenched teeth he said, "I've already explained several times. The golem needs to recognise you as its creator so that it will give its loyalty to you. It must be your hand that shapes those letters."

"I'll write them," I said. "Just tell me what they do."

Michael let out a long, heavy, drawn out from the tips of his toes to the top of his head, sigh. "*Abraq ad habra*," he said.

"Did you just say abracadabra?" I asked. "I thought that the Great Michael Scot was an alchemist not a fairy godmother from a Disney movie."

"Not abracadabra, *abraq ad habra*," he said. "It's Aramaic, an ancient language that has mostly been forgotten. It means 'I create with words'. The electricity will only be able to bring the golem to life if this word of power has been carved into its flesh."

It sounded like fairy-tale magic to me, but I didn't want to start Michael off on one of his speeches, so I picked up the stick. With him watching over my shoulder, I carefully carved the remaining letters into the golem's chest.

"Grand," said Michael, beaming. He pulled an ancient brass stethoscope out of his satchel, put its earpieces into his ears and pressed its bell onto the golem's chest.

"The heart isn't beating," I said.

"Shh," he said. "I'm trying to listen." He moved the stethoscope a few millimetres to the right.

I tapped Michael's shoulder to get his attention.

"You told me only electricity would bring it to life," I said loudly.

"If you can't be quiet, then go away," said Michael.

I sat, holding my questions in, watching as Michael covered every centimetre of the creature's huge, silent torso.

"Well?" I asked impatiently, as Michael straightened up and removed the ends of the stethoscope from his ears. "What were you listening to?"

"Everything in the universe vibrates," he explained. "If you listen closely enough you can hear it hum. The pitch and the rhythm of that hum can tell you about the nature of the thing you're listening to. If you know what you're doing," he added.

"So you were listening to the creature hum?" I asked doubtfully.

"Yes," said Michael. "And it's exactly as I thought." He shook his head slowly and sadly, like he was a doctor about to pronounce a lump of mud terminally dead. "You weren't frightened enough. There simply isn't enough ferociousness in the golem. If we brought it to life now, it'd wander down to the meadow and pet bunnies or pick wildflowers or do something else equally useless." An expression of complete disgust crossed his face.

Imagining a great big mud man sitting in a field of daisies petting a fluffy bunny made me smile. I'd have to draw the scene in my sketchbook when I got home.

"It's nothing to smile about," said Michael sulkily. "And don't you dare draw a picture of it being cuddly."

I frowned with what I hoped looked like sincere concern. "Of course not," I said. "So what do we need to do to give it a more – er – ferocious vibration?"

"Not we," said Michael, giving me one of his unnerving, unblinking stares. "You."

"Me?" I asked, startled. "But I don't know anything about magic – I mean alchemy," I corrected myself.

"You are the golem's creator," he said solemnly. "You are the only one who can influence its vibrations, its nature. I will of course continue to help in an advisory capacity, but you will have to do all the doing."

"Wow, that will be a big change," I said sarcastically. "So what does the Great Michael Scot advise me to do now?"

"Let's see," he said. "Spiders and flesh-eating plants don't work. What are you afraid of?"

"Pickled-frog juice?"

He just stared at me.

"Okay, okay," I said. "I'm afraid the burglars will come back when I'm there."

That thought seemed to cheer Michael up a bit. "That could work... if only we had something from one of the burglars."

"We do!" I said excitedly. I pulled out the straight piece of wool.

He shook his head. "We don't know for certain it came from a burglar. It's too risky."

"You mean, if this actually came from my sweater and I put it in the golem, he might hurt me?"

"You'd be fine," said Michael. "The golem will see you as its master no matter what, but that's not what I meant. If the wool is from some innocent party, then it will not help the golem become any more ferocious. Besides, there is a small possibility the golem could go after the person the thread came from, which would be unfortunate if it was from a child who had nothing to do with the burglary."

The wool had been found right outside the door to my garden. If any student of Hillside High School had been standing there, I doubted they were innocent, but I put the wool away.

"So for the golem to work it must be something I'm really scared of?" I said. Michael nodded. I took a deep breath. "I'm afraid of the dark," I said, my face flushing with embarrassment.

"The dark," said Michael, staring at me. "And how exactly do you propose to catch a piece of the dark?"

"I'm trying to help," I said.

"Unlike this poor fellow, you have a brain," said Michael, patting the golem's arm, "so use it."

Euan frightened me and I had something of his – the bit of knotted wool I'd taken from his jumper. But every time I mentioned Euan to anyone, they gave me the same boring lecture about standing up for myself, and I didn't feel like hearing it again, especially not from Michael, so I said nothing.

"Come on," said Michael. "Think. How about an animal?"

"A Rottweiler?" I asked.

Michael snorted. "You're lying. Rottweilers don't frighten you. Do you want to protect your home or not?"

"A bear," I said.

"A bear might do," said Michael. "But a real one, not one of those honey-eating saps they've got at the zoo." He paused, looking thoughtful. "The zoo is a good idea, though. What animal would you be the most terrified to be locked in a cage with?"

"What?" I said, alarmed. "I wouldn't get in a cage with any of them." Just how far would Michael take this crazy game of his?

"Ah good, you're finally getting scared," he said. "I was speaking hypothetically, of course, for pretend."

"I know what 'hypothetical' means," I snapped. "For pretend, then, let's see. Rhinos, with their armoured skins and their stubby but deadly horns – I would not want to be put in their pen." I remembered the warning signs by the African dogs. "Actually, no. That pair of striped African dogs, those are even scarier." Then I thought about the last time I'd been to the zoo. The way the male lion had flung back his head, opened his mouth and roared at his mate when she tried to sneak a bite of his dinner. "The lion."

"Are you sure?" asked Michael after I'd been silent for a moment. "You're not going to change your mind again?"

"No, I'm not," I said, thinking about the sketch I'd made of the scene, the long knife-like teeth and the razor-sharp claws. "Definitely the lion."

"Well, then," said Michael. "You've got to get something from a lion, a tooth or a claw maybe."

Now I knew how far Michael would take this: too far.

"Right, I'll just walk up to the enclosure and ask the nice lion to rip out one of his fangs and throw it to me across the double fence. Or were you thinking that I would go in and tear it out myself?"

"You're right," said Michael. "You're just a little girl. I should never—"

"Being small and being a girl have nothing to do with anything," I shouted. "It's too dangerous for anyone to go in a cage with a lion. If you're so brave and clever, why don't you go get a claw yourself?"

"I suppose it doesn't have to be a claw or a tooth," said Michael, backing down. "Anything that came from the lion would carry the vibration of its essence. Even a single strand of hair."

"Right, so now that it's you going after the bit of vibrating essence, a hair is fine," I said. "That figures."

I thought about the clumps of fur that fell off Henry every spring. "If you're lucky you might be able to find some just lying about on the path."

"Not me," said Michael placidly, "you. It's still got to be you."

I glanced at my watch. It was after four o'clock. Mum would be getting worried.

"Fine," I said. "But the zoo is closed. I'll have to go tomorrow morning."

Michael nodded curtly. "Make sure you hide the golem with leaves before you go," he said. His command given, he went off to mutter something to his frog.

I felt in my pocket and pulled out the piece of wool with the knot in it. As soon as Michael turned his back, I pressed it deep into the soil of the golem's belly. It might not be able to protect me at school, but I'd make sure Euan couldn't bother me at home or out here. Then I gathered leaves and dumped them over the golem until it was completely hidden. I was about to head home when I remembered Henry.

"Henry," I called, "you can come out now."

Nothing moved. I tugged on the leash. It slid through the undergrowth too easily. I pulled it out. Henry's empty collar dangled from the end.

## 13. EDDA AND THE LION

Michael told me, with a sniff, that he had more important things to do than look for a dog, so I searched the park on my own – being careful to stay on the paths this time. I shouted Henry's name, feeling worse and worse as the minutes ticked by. I searched for as long as I could, but at five o'clock I reluctantly turned towards home. My voice was hoarse from calling and a great big hollow had formed in the pit of my stomach. I wanted to keep looking, but Mum would be worrying about where I was.

Walking up to Mr Campbell's door holding Henry's empty collar was one of the hardest things I've ever done. I knew how much he loved that dog and my stomach churned at the thought of seeing the sadness on his face when I told him I'd lost Henry. Old-fashioned band music played cheerily on the stereo inside. I took a deep breath and pushed the bell. As soon as it rang I heard a bark from the side of the house and then a crash as a wheelie bin fell over. Henry came bounding out from behind it.

I crouched down and scratched his ears. "Were you hiding?" I asked.

He thumped his tail happily on the ground.

I heard the front door open behind me. I slipped the collar over Henry's head and stood up.

"Hi, Mr Campbell," I said. "Just bringing Henry home."

"I hope he was no trouble," he said.

"No," I said. "No trouble at all."

To my surprise Mum wasn't worried about me being late.

"You've made a new friend," she said, as I took off my coat. "He seems like a nice responsible boy."

"He does?" I asked, wondering if Michael had used some of his alchemy on her. Nice and responsible were not words I'd use.

"Is he friends with Lucy too?" she asked.

"Not really," I said, and then I groaned because I remembered I'd promised Lucy she could come over tomorrow. For half a second I thought about postponing my zoo quest, but now I'd made the golem I was impatient to finish bringing it to life.

After dinner I called Lucy and told her she couldn't come because my mum was taking me shopping to replace the presents the burglars had taken. It was a lie. Dad had just given me my new iPod – I had it open in my lap the whole time I was talking to her.

I felt bad as I hung up the phone – Lucy had sounded so disappointed – but I had to take care of the golem first. I would make it up to her as soon as the golem was alive. To make myself feel better, I got out my sketchbook and my pastels – I'd told my parents

I'd keep the set of birthday pastels, even if they were a bit battered – and drew the golem rampaging through the woods.

When I got up on Saturday morning, I found Mum and Dad in the kitchen, kitted out in their best boring clothes. Mum wore a plain grey skirt and a white blouse. Dad was crammed into his one and only suit.

"Why are you two so dressed up?" I asked, pulling a box of cereal out of the cupboard.

Mum looked guiltily at the mug of coffee in her hands before she answered, "We're going to look at some houses, just to get a feel for what's out there. I asked Mr Campbell if you can go round and play with Henry for a couple of hours."

"I'm busy," I said. "I'm going to the zoo with Michael – and his dad," I added. "School project."

"But we don't know Michael or his family very well," said Mum.

"I'm sure she'll be fine," said Dad. "Michael seems a sensible boy. Besides, all the dangerous beasties are locked away and there are always plenty of zoo keepers around."

"It's not the animals—" Mum began.

"Look at the time," Dad exclaimed with a wink to me. "We're going to be late," he said, hurrying her out the door.

Getting into the zoo ended up being more difficult than getting permission to go. I had to stand in a long queue for what seemed like the whole morning. When

I got to the front and plunked down my money, the woman behind the desk frowned, pointed to the sign above her head that read, "Under sixteens must be accompanied by an adult" and asked me how old I was.

I hastily pulled another five-pound note out of my pocket. "Sixteen," I said, standing as tall as I could without rising up on my tiptoes, and giving her the most sincere smile I could fake.

She didn't smile back. "Can I see some ID, please?" she asked. "Something with your date of birth on it."

"I don't have anything," I said truthfully.

"Then I'm sorry—" she began.

"I'm here with my dad," I said before she could finish. "He's parking the car. He told me to meet him by the sea-lion pool."

"I'm sorry, but you'll have to wait out here," she said, pointing to an empty bit of floor by the rack of leaflets.

"She's with me," said a familiar voice. I'd never been so happy to see Michael, although I had to wonder how he knew to come just when I needed him. Was he following me?

"Are you her father?" asked the woman doubtfully.

Michael laughed a fake, deep laugh – the kind that gets described in books as a chortle.

"No, no," he said. "I'm her older brother." He put the full adult entry fee on the counter next to mine. "Our father is parking the car."

"So I've heard," said the woman, but she took the money – including my extra five-pound note – and gave us our tickets.

"I can't believe I couldn't convince her I was sixteen," I fumed as soon as we were out of earshot.

"Well, you're not," said Michael unhelpfully.

I ignored him. "But she believed you were an adult and my brother."

Michael just grinned. "I got you in, didn't I?"

"Yeah, you did," I admitted grudgingly. "So does that mean you're going to help me after all?"

Before he had a chance to answer I heard someone call my name.

I looked around and my heart sank. Lucy was coming through the gate followed by her mother, aunt and five little cousins.

"Edda," said Lucy coming towards me, beaming, "it's great to see you, but I thought you had to go shopping today?"

"Um, Mum had to work," I said. "So, change of plans."

"Where's your dad?"

"Home," I said.

"Are you on your own?" Lucy asked, looking around. "You can always tag along with us."

She spotted Michael, who was lurking a few feet away. "Oh," she said. Her face took on that stiff look, like a mask, that she gets when her feelings are hurt and she's trying to hide it. "I guess you're still busy then."

I felt so bad, I kind of hoped a hole would open at my feet and swallow me up.

"I'm really sorry," I said. "It's just that there's something I have to do and Michael's helping me do it."

"That's okay," said Lucy. "I'm busy too. I guess I'll see you at school." Before I could say anything else she turned and followed her family to the flamingo pond. As soon as I'd sorted things out, I was going to have to do something really nice for her or I wouldn't have a best friend much longer.

"Come on," I said to Michael. "Let's get this over with."

"I'm sorry," he said, "but I have business elsewhere."

"But you came..." I said.

"You thought I came here to help you?" he said.

"Well, yeah. You helped me before. You knew I was going to the zoo, you showed up just in time..."

Michael chortled again. "Purely coincidental. I came by the zoo to have a chat with Corax." He must have seen the disbelief written on my face. "The raven," he added. "He keeps me informed about politics."

"Politics?" I asked. This was becoming his lamest excuse ever.

"Yes," said Michael. "He lets me know the latest news from the Parliament of Birds. They're always in a squabble about something. Usually about who gets to be king."

"Right," I said. "That sounds exciting. Tell Corax I said hello."

Michael nodded solemnly and headed off in the direction of the raven cage.

I hesitated, wondering if I should go after Lucy, explain everything, apologise and beg her not to be angry with me. But if I told her what I was doing here, she'd probably think I was as crazy as Michael, so I took the path marked "Asiatic lions" instead.

A line of bushes separated the path from the lions' fence. As the lions prowled hungrily around the boundaries of their enclosure, I walked slowly along the path, my eyes fixed on the ground, searching for hairs. I went all the way up to the lion house and all the way back down again without finding anything.

I looked at the bushes. Any hair that blew through the fence would probably get caught in their leaves and branches. I didn't see a sign saying, "Stick to the path" so I decided to investigate, pushing my way into a clump of rhododendrons.

As I got closer to the fence, the she lion caught sight of me. Her tail twitching, she pinned me with her yellow-eyed glare. I knew two fences stood between us, but the hairs on the back of my neck rose up anyway. She leapt, charging towards me across the ground faster than I could have believed possible. I held my breath. At the last minute she turned and slowed to a saunter, continuing her walk along the fence with her tail held high. Released from her terrifying gaze, my whole body went weak and wobbly.

"Hey!" someone shouted. "Come away from there." I turned. A keeper was driving up the path in an electric cart. "You shouldn't antagonise the lions," she said, as I stumbled out of the rhododendrons.

"Sorry," I said. "I didn't mean to." As if a mouse could ever antagonise a lion. "I just wanted a closer view."

The keeper seemed to accept my excuse. "Hop in," she said. "I'm taking them their lunch. You'll be able to get a good view through the window in the lion house."

I sat silently on the short ride, trying to get up the

nerve to ask for a favour. The keeper parked by a door marked "No Public Access" and heaved a big cooler off the back of the cart. It was my last chance.

"Um..." I began, "would you be able to get me a lion hair?" I asked.

She raised an eyebrow questioningly, but she didn't say no.

"It's for a science project," I said, using Michael's standard half-truth. "I want to compare different animal hairs under a microscope."

"That sounds interesting," she said. "But I never go anywhere near the lions. They're too dangerous. You saw how quickly they move."

Exactly what I had told Michael. "But doesn't it fall off, like a dog's?" I asked. "Could you get some that was just lying around?"

She laughed. "Those poor lions are from India," she said. "And it's coming towards wintertime. They're holding onto every single hair they've got. Sorry."

I left the keeper and walked around to the public viewing area. I watched through the large window as she dragged a couple of hunks of raw meat into the empty lion house. The lions, catching a whiff of their dinner, began to yowl hungrily in the background.

As soon as she was safely out of the straw-covered room, the keeper released the gates and the lions came bounding in. Each grabbed a haunch and dragged it to a separate corner to feed.

The male lion tore off chunks of meat with vicious enthusiasm, but the lioness didn't seem to like her food. She started eyeing her mate's. He caught her watching and raised his bloody snout, growling a warning that sent a shiver down my spine. She didn't seem discouraged. She started slinking towards him. Just like last time, he threw his head back and roared. The sound was so loud the window in front of me shook. I touched it lightly, feeling the glass vibrate against my skin.

That was it!

Michael said we needed something that carried the vibration of a ferocious beast. I knew from school that sound is just air vibrating, so wouldn't the lion's roar be full of his essence?

I dug in my bag and pulled out my iPod. It had a tiny microphone built into it. It took me a few minutes to figure out how to record. By that time the female lion had settled down again, but her patience was short. She seemed convinced her mate had the tastier meal.

My finger hovered over the screen as she got up and started creeping towards him again. Each time he raised his head, she dropped to her haunches and looked away, pretending she wasn't interested, but eventually she snuck all the way around behind him. She waited for him to take a bite and then she pounced on his meat. He sprang up, whirled on her, his claws extended, and roared.

I hit record just in time.

Bubbling with excitement at having finished my second quest all by myself in what must be record time, I practically floated down the path to the raven cage. Michael wasn't there. The raven hopped over to me and croaked, but I couldn't understand what he was trying to tell me.

I decided to go find Michael at his tower. I left the zoo and walked along Corstorphine Road to an iron gate identical to the one at the end of my street. I looked around, just to make sure my parents weren't driving by – they weren't – unlatched the gate, and slipped inside. I followed the steep path up through a small stand of trees and out onto the rabbit meadow Henry loved so much. The image of a huge, ferocious golem sitting in the sun, surrounded by bunnies, popped into my head and I couldn't help grinning to myself.

When I got to the tower, the door was unlocked. I went inside, pulled the mouldy mat off the trapdoor, and knocked on it.

No one answered.

I hauled it open. The stone steps spiralled down into perfect darkness.

"Michael," I called. "Are you down there?"

No reply.

As I felt my way down into the darkness, step by step, I wished I'd brought a torch with me. The deeper I went, the less light reached me from above, until eventually I was in complete blackness. I waved my hand in front of my eyes. Nothing. What if someone shut the trapdoor and put something heavy on it, trapping me down here? I hesitated. Part of me wanted to turn around and bolt for freedom. *Don't be silly*, I told myself. *Michael would only leave the door unlocked if he was here.*

"Michael?" I called, my voice coming out as a squeak.

A door creaked open below and my hands and feet emerged out of the darkness. I raced down the last dozen stairs.

"Did you get it?" asked Michael, looking up from the book he was reading.

"Yeah," I said, showing him my iPod.

"That doesn't look like it came from a lion," he said.

"You have to put these on." I passed him the headphones. He put them on and I pressed play.

As he listened, a smile spread across his face. He took off the headphones.

"Sound is a vibration," I said. "I remembered that when I heard the lion roar."

"It's a very clever idea," he said. A warm glow of pride spread through my belly. "Shall we go see if it works?"

I waited impatiently as Michael put away his book and got out his satchel. "Don't go anywhere," he said to Benedict, who was squatting in his jar on the table. Michael picked up the lantern and led the way back up the stairs.

Michael made us take a new route to the golem's clearing: "We don't want to trample a path and have curious gawkers follow it."

He helped me pull off all the leaves and then he had me put the headphones around the golem's head. I hadn't given the golem any ears so I had to guess where to put them. I hit play.

Michael got out his stethoscope and listened to the golem's chest. He frowned and moved it to another position.

"Play that again," he said. I hit play, watching Michael anxiously as his frown deepened.

"Isn't it working?" I asked.

"The roar is working fine," he said, still frowning, "but there are other fears vibrating through the golem that I didn't hear yesterday. They don't seem to have anything to do with lions."

I thought of the wool I'd pushed into the golem's body. "Can you tell what kind of fears?" I asked nervously.

He shook his head. "If I had the object it came from, I could match it, but no, I can't read it from the golem. You didn't change anything, did you?"

"When could I have done that?" I asked instead of answering. I didn't want to admit what I'd done and have Michael make fun of me for being afraid of Euan. "Will the golem still work?"

"Oh, it'll work, all right," he said. "It certainly possesses enough fear now. But without knowing exactly where it all came from, it will be less predictable." He stared at me unblinking. I had the feeling he knew I was lying. I pretended to be busy brushing off the few remaining leaves.

"So what next?" I asked, hoping to change the topic.

"All it needs now is the spark of life," said Michael. "He pulled a large spool of plastic-coated wire out of his apparently bottomless satchel and handed me the end. "Put this in its solar plexus," he said.

"The solar what?" I asked.

"The point between its chest and its abdomen," said Michael, placing his hand just below his own ribcage to demonstrate. "The power centre of all vertebrates."

The golem didn't have any ribs or even a stomach, so I took a guess and stuck the wire into the middle of its body.

"Stick a rock on top to stop it from being pulled out," said Michael, unwinding more wire.

I plunked a nice big round stone on top of the golem's solar plexus, covered the creature with leaves again and followed Michael as he headed back to the tower, unwinding wire as he went.

When I caught up, he was standing at the edge of the woods watching an old man walk by with a springer spaniel. The dog was straining to get as far from Michael as his leash would allow, and his owner, who hadn't seen Michael, was struggling to keep control. I was about to ask how we were going to get electricity – I hadn't seen a power point in Michael's room – when I realised we were facing the radio tower. It stood opposite the stone tower, protected by a three-metre tall fence covered in warning signs. My heart filled with dread.

"We're not going in there, are we?" I asked, a "Danger of Death" sign staring me in the face.

Michael looked where I was pointing. "Why would we do that?" he asked, pulling a long knife out of his satchel.

"Electricity," I said quietly, afraid of giving Michael any ideas.

"Too risky," said Michael, shaking his head. "They have closed circuit television networks in there. They might spot you. We'll use my tower. It's been struck by lightning before." He crouched down and plunged his knife into the ground. "Make sure the wire goes in," he said. He began cutting a narrow trench towards the tower. I followed behind, stomping the wire in, to hide it from view.

When we reached the tower, Michael pulled a ball of string out of his satchel, tossed it to me and sent me up to the roof with it. Once again the view held me breathless. Even though it was a grey day and the clouds hung low in the sky, I could still see as far as Fife, where it was raining. I could see tankers making their way up the Firth of Forth, and the misty slopes of the Pentland Hills.

"Hurry up," Michael called in a low voice.

I held onto one end of the string and dropped the rest down to the tiny figure of Michael below. He tied the spool to the string and I hauled it up. There was just enough wire for me to wrap it a couple of times around the tower's shiny lightning rod. I peered more closely at the rod. The screws that attached it to the roof were rusty, so it wasn't as new as it looked. I'd been in Edinburgh for just over a year and I could only remember one thunderstorm, and that had been in the middle of winter. Did thunderstorms even happen in the autumn?

"Uh, Michael," I called down as loudly as I dared. "When was the tower hit by lightning?"

"1914," he replied confidently.

"Does your *Book of Might* have a recipe for calling up a storm?" I asked. "Or are you just hoping we'll get lucky."

"I see your point," he said.

I was shocked and a little pleased to discover that the Great Michael Scot could make mistakes. But then he turned to survey the radio tower and my heart sank. There had to be a less dangerous way of getting electricity. A gust of wind blew my hair in front of my face and I had an idea. If there's one thing you can count on in Edinburgh, it's wind.

"Hang on," I called. "I'm coming down."

Michael listened, his eyebrows knotted together, as I tried to explain wind turbines to him. After about ten minutes his eyes finally brightened. "Ah, you mean use a windmill to turn a generator," he said. "Another clever idea," he said. "You might have the makings of an alchemist after all."

I was so surprised by the compliment, I stood there stunned, my mouth hanging open, while Michael bolted down his tower hole muttering to himself. By the time I followed him downstairs, he'd already pulled a hundred bits and pieces off the shelves, and dumped them on the table.

"Hold this," he said, thrusting an old metal pinwheel into my hands. "And here's a magnet," he said, dropping it into my other hand. "I'll just solder it onto the pinwheel." He held a piece of iron into the lantern flame until it was red hot and then came towards me, brandishing it like a sword. I backed up, banging into the table. "Hold still," he said, "or I'll get molten metal all over you."

I held still as he attached the magnet to the pinwheel.

"There, that should do it," he said, giving it a spin.

Then he took a long piece of copper wire and coiled it so that the magnet was free to spin inside. "See, the pinwheel turns the magnet which gets the electrons in the wire moving. Now we just need to fix it all to the golem's wire."

Michael raced up the steps two at a time with me puffing along behind on my shorter legs, still gripping the makeshift wind turbine.

He used some more solder to attach the golem's wire to the copper coil and then we mounted the whole contraption onto the ramparts above the stairwell.

"Now all we need is some wind," said Michael, giving me a wicked grin.

A breeze blew by. I looked hopefully at the pinwheel. It made one slow rotation and then stopped.

"We're going to need a lot more than that," said Michael. "But this is Edinburgh, so I'm sure we won't have to wait long."

Doing something to protect my house and family made me feel stronger, braver, bigger. Saturday night, for the first time since the robbery, I fell asleep with the lights out.

I did not sleep long.

That night, a storm blew in from the west. It rattled my window, waking me from uneasy dreams of whirling tornadoes and sinister footsteps.

I lay under my duvet, listening to the racket outside. I imagined the blades of the pinwheel chasing each other furiously round and round, sending a stream of electricity down the wire, under the ground, and into the golem. "The pulse of life," Michael had called it.

A gust of wind hit the window like a giant fist and howled around the walls seeking a way in. I switched on the bedside lamp and sat up, drawing my knees to my chest and pulling the duvet up to my chin.

How much electricity did the golem need to come alive, I wondered, and how long would it take the creature to lumber down here to my house?

I imagined its blank eyes blinking open, gazing at the waving treetops high above. In my mind it lurched to its feet and staggered through the undergrowth towards my house. With its thick skin of mud, and its strong arms and legs, it would be able to stride straight through the bramble bushes.

For all I knew the wind might have been blowing for a couple of hours. The golem might already be standing guard on the other side of the wall, watching over our bungalow while we slept. The idea made me feel warm and safe. I didn't have to worry about burglars any more.

I snuggled down under my duvet and fell back to sleep.

# 14. SAFE AT LAST

"What's wrong with Henry?" Dad asked Mr Campbell across the short box hedge that separated our two back gardens. The wind had blown all the clouds away, leaving a clear, deep-blue sky behind. I was helping Dad rake up the leaves and branches that had been thrown about the lawn. Henry was whining pitifully at Mr Campbell's back door, begging to be let inside.

"He's been playing up since early this morning," said Mr Campbell. "Normally he sleeps through a storm, but this one's got him rattled. He paced up and down the hall all night. When I finally got up, he didn't want to go outside. I had to push him out. He did his business lickety-split, right next to the house, and dashed back in. I thought he'd be better with me outside with him, but no."

"Is he sick?" asked Dad. "I can run the two of you down to the vet's if you need me to."

"Ach, no," said Mr Campbell. "He's spooked is all, but I'll be darned if I know what did it."

I looked towards the trees of the nature reserve. They seemed unnaturally still now the wind had gone.

Was the golem out there? Could Henry smell him? Was that what was bothering him, or was he still upset about being dragged into the woods yesterday?

Last night I'd felt certain the golem had come alive, but it's easier to believe in things after dark. Could the strange letters, the little turbine, the bits of plants and the lion's roar have really brought mud to life?

"Was Henry acting strangely yesterday after I brought him home?" I asked.

"No," said Mr Campbell. "He was fine until the storm. Don't worry yourself, it's nothing you've done."

I wasn't so sure.

Henry looked over at me with his big, sad, brown eyes, rose up on his hind legs and scratched at the door.

"I made him to protect us," I whispered.

"What was that?" asked Dad.

"Nothing," I said. I went inside.

I needed to know if the golem had actually come to life. The best way to do that would be to go back to the clearing where I'd left it, but there was no way I'd go on my own, even if Mum let me. Michael promised the golem wouldn't hurt me, but the idea of being in the woods when a two-and-a-half-metre-tall man made out of mud might be walking around was a little bit, well, scary.

If only I had a way to contact Michael, but I didn't even know where his house was. He seemed to spend most of his time at the tower anyway, but looking for him there would mean going to the park alone.

I could always call Lucy. She was the most practical, dependable person I'd ever met and she wanted to know what I'd been doing. If I showed her, that might make up for cancelling on her yesterday, and then she could tell me if all this was just in my imagination.

Lucy sounded happy to hear from me when I phoned, which made me feel like an even worse friend for lying to her before. I told her I had something to show her, something I'd made.

"Will it be just us two?" she asked. Could she actually be jealous of Michael? The idea made me feel pleased but awkward and uncomfortable all at the same time.

"Of course," I replied.

She came as promised, right after lunch.

The afternoon was sunny and warm. Corstorphine Hill Nature Reserve was full of couples and families and people walking their dogs. In the bright sunlight, with Lucy by my side, the idea that ground up bits of plant and a trickle of electricity could bring a pile of mud to life seemed silly. I was too embarrassed to admit what Michael had got me to believe. I decided I'd take her to the clearing. If the golem was gone, I'd tell her everything. If it was still there, I'd tell her I'd made a sculpture.

I stopped at the tower and crouched by the door to check the wire. It was still in place.

"What's that for?" asked Lucy.

It was my chance to tell her everything. I chickened out. "You'll see," was all I could say.

As I followed the wire, invisible now beneath the ground, my nervousness returned. What if it had worked? The thought wasn't comforting any more.

What if Michael decided to help someone else make a golem, someone like Euan? There could be golems everywhere.

Up ahead, I could see the bushes that circled the clearing. Suddenly I didn't want to know the truth; it might be too scary. I stopped. Lucy banged into me.

"We should just go home," I said.

My fear must have shown on my face because Lucy gave me an odd sort of look, crossed her arms over her chest and said, "No. You've been acting strangely all week, ever since... Look, you dragged me here. I'm not going anywhere until you tell me exactly what's going on."

When Lucy gets fierce and determined like that, it's impossible to change her mind.

"I made a gol— a man out of dirt," I said, "and left it over there." I pointed to the clearing.

"You mean like a sculpture?" Lucy asked.

She'd said that she wanted the truth. "No," I said. "Not a sculpture, an actual man."

Lucy raised her eyebrow. I knew she didn't believe me, but she didn't say anything.

"Well, I mean yes, I did sculpt it out of mud," I continued, feeling the need to fill the silence. "Michael had this list of plants we had to... I had to collect..."

"Which is why you didn't finish the scavenger hunt," said Lucy.

I nodded. "And then he said I had to get something from the zoo that carried the essence of ferociousness..."

Lucy's other eyebrow went up. She was right; it sounded ridiculous.

"Edda," said Lucy gently, "he was playing a practical joke on you."

I thought about Michael. He had no sense of humour. "No," I said. "He believed in it too and you haven't seen his room in the tower. He has all these old books and potions and other weird stuff."

"But you can't just bring something to life with plants and whatever you got from the zoo…"

"A lion's roar," I said quietly, hearing how silly it sounded. I already knew what Lucy thought about me letting Euan bother me, so I didn't mention the thread.

"Honestly, Edda, you can't believe—"

"And electricity," I added. "The plants and the roar were just to make it scary. The electricity was supposed to actually give it life." I told her about the wire and the wind turbine. She was unimpressed.

"It's been done before," I said, telling her what I'd read on the internet.

"But those were just stories," said Lucy.

"They were legends," I replied, "and legends are usually based on something that really happened. Mrs Doak said so when we studied William Wallace."

"Maybe, but I don't think the monster bit was the true part," said Lucy. "You're letting your imagination run away with you."

The more Lucy said it couldn't be true, the more I wanted it to be true. I wanted the golem to be alive.

"There's only one way to find out," I said, walking towards the clearing.

I stopped at its edge. A huge man-shaped hollow

spread out before me, the wire dangling into its emptiness.

"I thought you said you made a sculpture," said Lucy. "This is a hole."

"That's where I made the golem, where I left it yesterday afternoon. It's alive. It got up and walked away." I felt a rush of mixed-up feeling. I felt excited and even a bit proud that I had created something so amazing, but at the same time, my heart raced and my palms sweated with a smidgeon of fear. Knowing things like this were possible, that mud could get up and walk away, changed everything.

"There are other explanations," said Lucy, cutting into my thoughts. "Michael could have come back here after you left and dug this hole to make you think his golem came to life."

"Not *his* golem," I said. "*My* golem. He made me do everything so the golem would be loyal to me." My house would be safe now.

"See," said Lucy, "like I said before, he was having fun with you, making you do silly things for no reason."

Lucy's refusal to listen was beginning to annoy me.

"Where did he put all the dirt then?" I asked. "It's a big hole."

"He could have carted it off in a wheelbarrow. There's lots of old wells on this hill," said Lucy.

I shook my head. "The nearest is at least ten minutes away and I don't see any wheel marks, do you? Besides, Michael is the laziest person I know. He wouldn't do all that just to play a joke."

"He got someone else to do it then," said Lucy. "Look at all the stuff he got you to do."

She walked carefully around the edge of the hole and over to a trampled bush. "See," she said, "a wheelbarrow could have done that."

Or a golem. I went over to take a look. A trail of broken undergrowth led from the clearing.

"There are still no wheel marks," I said. I spotted an oval-shaped depression in the ground. I grabbed Lucy's arm. "Look, a footprint!" I stepped into it. It was at least three times as big as my boot.

"It doesn't look like a footprint," said Lucy doubtfully.

"I didn't give the golem any toes," I said. "The soil was too crumbly. Look, there's another one."

We followed the trail of footprints through the woods, each one and a half metres from the last. Seeing the size of them and remembering how large I'd made the golem, I began to feel uneasy. Had the spell worked? Would the golem be loyal to me? The trail ended at the path that led to the tower.

"The ground is too packed down here," I said, "but it looks like the golem was heading towards my house."

"Or to the tower," said Lucy, "which you said Michael has keys to, right? So, Michael dug out the hole and then on his way back to the tower he made the trail."

"Why won't you believe me?" I asked angrily.

"I know you want to believe something's protecting your house and family," said Lucy, looking apologetic. "It must be awful to have things stolen, especially on your birthday, but bringing mud to life is impossible."

"You don't know anything about anything," I said. "Michael is helping me. He understands."

"It's always Michael," said Lucy, her black eyes

flashing. "You only met him a few days ago and now you believe everything he tells you. He's a bully, just like Euan, only you don't notice because he's pretending to be on your side."

"He's nothing like Euan," I said, "and he's not pretending."

"Right," said Lucy. "So he never told you to do something that could get you in trouble or put you in danger?"

I thought about sneaking into the greenhouses and how his eyes had lit up when he told me to find a lion's claw. But if I admitted Lucy was right about that, I'd also have to admit I could be wrong about the golem. I refused to do that.

"You're just jealous," I said.

"Why, because I'm not a pretentious know-it-all like Michael who only comes to school to show off?" said Lucy.

"That's not what I meant," I said. I wanted her to say she was jealous because I'd been spending time with Michael instead of her.

"Okay," said Lucy. "Suppose it's true. Suppose a thirteen-year-old boy in Scotland somehow knows how to do something no scientist can do and he decides to share it with a girl he's just met. How does having a giant monster running around in the woods behind her house make that girl safer?"

"The golem won't hurt me because I'm its maker," I said.

"Says who?" Lucy asked. "Michael? Making a monster didn't work out so well for Dr Frankenstein.

What happened in those legends you read?"

"It worked out all right," I said. I remembered the one story where the golem had turned bad. "Mostly. At least the rabbi, the man who made it, was okay."

Lucy looked sceptical.

"So are you saying you believe me now?" I asked.

"No. Edda, as your friend I'm telling you it's not possible. I'm trying to make you see that Michael isn't your friend."

We walked out of the park without saying much to each other. Lucy kept trying to start a conversation, but I didn't feel like talking. I'd never had a best friend before, but I thought they should believe you, no matter what.

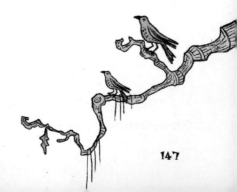

## 15. A PAIR OF HEDGEHOGS

I woke. Some noise had pulled me out of my sleep. My ears were straining so hard to hear it, I felt like they might actually be growing bigger. The wind rustled through the leaves of the trees. At first the thumping sound was so low I thought it was my heart beating nervously in my chest, but then it stopped and my heart raced on. I looked at the clock; it was just past midnight. I held my breath, waiting. A minute ticked by.

*Thump. Thump. Thump.*

It was closer now. The bed shook with the sound. I felt the impact in my bones, as if someone outside had pulled up a tree and was pounding the ground with it – or as if something with tree-trunk legs was walking towards the house. I sat bolt upright.

The golem was coming. I shivered and pulled the duvet up to my chin, telling myself that a great big monster with a heart made of cactus spines and cobwebs was a good thing. It was what I'd wanted: protection. But now, alone in bed in the dark, I didn't feel safe. I felt more afraid than ever.

Lucy's question burned in my mind: did bringing a monster to life really make me safer? Michael said it would recognise me, but what if something had gone wrong? Or what if Lucy was right and Michael wasn't really my friend?

A cold trickle of fear ran down my back as the thumping drew closer. I thought about how tall I'd made it, how thick its arms and legs were. I'd built it strong enough to crash through anything, even a stone wall.

I wanted to turn on the light, to chase the dark shadows away, but I was afraid the lit window would attract the golem, just like it attracted moths. I shrank down under the duvet, squeezed my eyes tightly shut, and tried to pretend nothing was happening, while I listened for the explosion of masonry and rock.

But the thudding eventually stopped and the explosion never came. I must have drifted back to sleep because the next thing I knew the alarm was buzzing. I opened my eyes. The dull daylight of another drizzly day crept in under the curtains.

I lay in bed, trying to make sense of it all. The golem must exist. I'd seen its footprints yesterday. I'd heard it walking last night. Hadn't I? Had it come into the back garden? Was it out there now?

I slipped out of bed, ran over to the window and pulled the curtains open. It was a miserably grim day, but the garden looked the same as ever and the wall was still standing. The boards across the door were still in place, and anyway, even if it had been unbarred, the door was too small to let the golem through. Could it climb over the wall?

I closed the curtains and threw on my school uniform. I could hear Mum clattering about the kitchen and smell the familiar morning smell of her coffee, but I headed to the back door instead. I needed to know if the golem had been here. I pulled my wellies on over my tights and went outside.

The wet air left beads of water on my navy jumper as I trudged across the garden. No golem-sized footprints broke the surface of the overgrown lawn, so it hadn't been in the garden. Had it been here at all? Could it still be lurking in the wilderness beyond the wall, waiting and watching? Part of me wanted proof that I was right, that I had made a golem and it had come to life, but another part of me was terrified at the idea of coming face to face with the monster.

If the door hadn't been nailed shut, I could have stuck my head out and checked. I looked at my father's shed. If I climbed onto the roof I might be able to see over.

I got one foot up on the windowsill and grabbed hold of the drainpipe, trying to remember if Michael had said anything about the golem sleeping. Did it find somewhere to hide during the day? What would happen if someone walking their dog came across it? I hoped Michael would be at school today so I could ask him all my questions.

My foot slipped off the windowsill and I stumbled backwards. My heel caught on something soft but crunchy. Startled, I jumped back, lost my balance entirely and fell hard on the soggy grass, my face only a couple of centimetres away from the curled-up bodies of two dead hedgehogs.

Stifling a scream, I scrambled to my feet and ran back inside.

I changed out of my wet, muddy clothes and into clean ones. Mum had made me toast, but when I bit into it, it felt crunchy and squishy in exactly the same way the dead hedgehog had felt under my foot. Gagging, I spat it out. Luckily, Mum didn't see; she was in her bedroom getting dressed for work. I threw my uneaten toast into the rubbish bin and bolted out the front door before she could catch me skipping breakfast.

I needed to speak to Michael, but when I got to school neither he nor his bike were there. The only other person I could ask for help – my only other friend – was Lucy. Maybe she would believe me now. I headed for the library. If I was lucky, she'd be working on an assignment.

I groaned: my history assignment! I'd completely forgotten about it. As if the golem wasn't bad enough, now I was going to be in trouble with Mrs Doak.

Lucy sat in the library reading a book. She was the only one there besides Mr Bradbury. I hesitated at the door. She hadn't believed me yesterday. Why would she be any different today?

Just then, Lucy looked up, saw me and smiled. A weight lifted off me. I wasn't alone. Even if she didn't believe me, she'd still be my friend, and she'd still try to help.

In a whispered voice, I told her what I'd heard last night and how I'd found the dead hedgehogs. Mr Bradbury glowered at us. I turned my back on him and spoke more quietly.

"It's all my fault they died," I said. "I feel terrible. I should never have made the golem."

"There's nothing for you to feel bad about," Lucy whispered back. "You didn't do anything, because there is no golem. The thumping was probably two branches knocking together and a cat could have killed the hedgehogs. Michael's the one who should be blamed."

"Shhh," Mr Bradbury hissed. Lucy blushed and looked down at her book.

I wanted to point out that if it was just the wind and a cat, Michael couldn't be blamed, but talking about him seemed to make us angry with each other. Besides, I didn't want to get Lucy in trouble with the librarian.

"I'll see you in class," I whispered.

I was disappointed she hadn't believed me. But she hadn't heard what I'd heard. Branches bumping together didn't get louder like the thumping had. But it was more than that. I had this feeling of certainty deep down inside me that the golem existed. Maybe it was the link Michael talked about. If I could get Lucy to come with me to the tower after school, I knew Michael would convince her of the truth.

As I left, the bell rang. The library was next to the gymnasium at the end of a long hall without lockers. All the other students were flooding in through the main doors and heading for their classes, so I was alone – until Euan came out of the boys' toilets. Instead of going to class, he turned towards me.

I glanced back, hoping Lucy had appeared, but the hallway was empty. My feet wanted to turn around and march back into the library. Euan wouldn't dare do anything in front of a teacher. But I forced myself to stay put. If I wanted to be more than a mouse, I had to start acting differently. This was my chance to prove I wasn't scared of Euan Morrison. After all, I knew things he didn't know, like the fact I had a golem to protect me – at least when I was on Corstorphine Hill, which wouldn't do me any good right now. I retreated a couple of steps.

Euan was kicking a crumpled crisp packet along the floor. He looked more surly than usual: his head hung down, and his shoulders slumped forward. As he came closer I could see why. The skin around his eye was a sickly reddish-purple, swollen half shut, his eye reduced to a slit.

I thought about the blue thread of wool I'd taken from his jumper and stuck inside the golem. Had Euan gone mountain biking yesterday? Had the golem hunted him down and walloped him? I should have felt happy. After all, I'd wished for something like this to happen since the day Euan had stolen my mouse drawing. But instead I felt sick.

"What are you looking at, you little freak?" said Euan, catching sight of me.

I knew I had to get out of his way. The longer I stood rooted in place, staring, the more serious the consequences would be. But I couldn't move; the sight of his puffy red eye mesmerised me.

"Are you looking for trouble?" he asked, straightening up to his full height – at least a foot taller than me. "Cos I could give you your own black eye. That way you wouldn't have to stare at mine."

To my surprise, an actual response sprang into my head: *How could I stare at my own eye?* But I didn't say it out loud.

"Do – you – understand – English?" Euan asked, dragging the words out.

It was a lame thing to say. Lucy was right; he was a pathetic bully. I knew exactly how I'd draw this scene: me tall and queenly wearing a horned Viking helmet, towering over Euan the one-eyed troll. I'd put the golem somewhere in the background of the picture, my loyal knight. I couldn't help myself, a grin slipped out.

Euan scowled, shoved me half-heartedly into the wall and stalked down the hall.

"Are you okay?" asked Lucy, rushing up to me.

I nodded. He hadn't pushed me hard enough to hurt. In fact, I was more than okay.

"You were right," I said to Lucy and smiled. "I'm not going to let him bother me any more."

She smiled back in a puzzled sort of way.

## 16. CONSEQUENCES

At first it felt fabulous to be the new Edda, no longer afraid of mediocre bullies like Euan. I answered questions in class. At lunch I sat with Lucy, Beth and Christine and I discovered I had things to talk about with them. We laughed like we'd been friends for years. But every time I saw Euan, he looked more and more miserable. The sick feeling I'd had when I first saw his swollen eye returned.

Euan stayed inside at lunch, even though his friends Murdo and George came out to kick around a football. As our afternoon class wore on, he sank lower and lower in his chair, until only his head and shoulders showed above his desk. I knew that look: he was hoping to disappear.

Euan was mean. He'd picked me as a taunting target from the first moment he saw me, but he never actually physically hurt me; mostly he just made fun of me, which meant I was worse than he was. Bullying was bullying, whether you did it yourself or magicked up a great big mud-monster to do it for you.

I glanced at Euan again. He was staring bleakly at his

blank notebook page. Wouldn't he be in worse shape if the golem had attacked him? After all, I'd made the monster almost twice his size. Maybe Lucy was right about the hedgehogs. Maybe they'd been killed by a cat. And maybe Euan had run into a branch on his mountain bike. But even if the golem hadn't given Euan the black eye, it didn't make me any less guilty. When I'd put the thread from his jumper into the golem's flesh, I'd already believed Michael could bring it to life and I'd wanted this to happen.

The most confusing part was that my fear of Euan had gone. I'd done something terrible and it had worked. I'd got my wish. I remembered imagining Euan as a troll and myself as the conquering queen. I thought about the grin that had snuck across my face. To him, it must have looked like I was smirking at his pain. I buried my face in my hands, feeling something worse than embarrassment – shame – and laid my head on my desk.

"Edda, are we keeping you from your beauty sleep?" asked Mrs Philpotts.

"Sorry," I said, straightening up. "Headache." It wasn't a complete lie. While I had no physical pain, the thoughts chasing each other around my mind hurt in a different way. For the rest of the afternoon I tried to ignore them, doing my best to stay focused on the lesson.

I needed to talk to Michael. I needed to tell him about the terrible thing I'd done with the wool from Euan's jumper and make him undo it before someone got badly injured. If he wasn't going to come to school any more, then I would go find him at his tower. Happily, Lucy agreed to come with me.

She chattered away as we walked up Hillside Drive, but I didn't hear much of what she said. I was too busy feeling bad about Euan and worrying about going into the park. Even if the golem had nothing to do with the dead hedgehogs or Euan's eye, I had made it big enough and strong enough to hurt people. I kept thinking about the version of the story in which the Prague golem had turned on those it was meant to protect. I might not be afraid of Euan any more, but the golem was starting to scare me. Was this what Michael meant when he said, "Be careful what you wish for"?

"So, what do you think?" Lucy asked.

I had no idea what she was talking about. I stared at her blankly.

"You haven't heard a word I've said, have you?"

I shook my head sheepishly.

Lucy sighed. "You're not still thinking about the golem, are you? As soon as we find Michael I'm going to make him confess it was all a trick."

I doubted even Lucy could make Michael do something he didn't want to do. It was a depressing thought. How was I going to get him to fix the golem?

But as we turned onto my road, all thoughts of Michael were chased from my head by the sight of a police car squatting outside my house. My heart pounded in my chest. What had happened? Had the burglars returned, like the policeman said they would? Or had something worse happened? What if the golem had attacked one of my parents?

I looked at Lucy. Her eyes were as wide as mine.

"Do you want me to come in with you?" she asked as we got to my house. I loved her for asking, but I thought about how exposed I'd felt last time we'd been broken into. It would be worse with someone else there. I shook my head.

"Call me," she said, as I went up the steps to my door.

"Definitely," I said. I watched her turn and walk away.

*I am Edda the Brave*, I told myself, *I can face anything*. But I didn't believe it. I took a deep breath, pushed open the door and stepped inside.

The sound of laughter and – stranger still – of teacups clinking against saucers floated down the hallway. Surprised, I followed the noise into the living room. I found my parents sitting on a sofa facing the beefy policeman, who was balancing a cup and saucer precariously on his knee as he ate a Jaffa Cake. I blinked. The cup was one of the ones the burglars had taken.

"Ah, there she is," said Mum, waving me forward with a smile. "Officer Carlisle came by to return some of the things that were stolen." She held out a jewellery box. "Happy birthday," she said.

Hands shaking with relief, I took the box. It was the one I'd found on the floor a week ago, the one with the crest of the Kirkcaldy jeweller on it. I opened it. Inside was a gold watch with a slender leather band.

"Hold out your hand," said Mum.

I obeyed. Mum took off my old scratched-up, plastic watch and fastened on the new one. It made my wrist look grown-up.

"From Nana Macdonald," Mum said.

"I saw the box," I said. "The watch is beautiful," I added, worried I'd sounded rude, but I had other things on my mind. I turned to Officer Carlisle. "Did you catch them?"

He nodded, his mouth full of biscuit. "Picked them up a couple of days ago," he said, after he'd swallowed. "But we had to record the goods before we could return them. Your drawing was very helpful. Quite the little artist you've got here," he said to my parents.

My face flushed. I'd forgotten Dad had photocopied one of my sketches to show the police what Great-Granny Macdonald's dinner service looked like. The idea of a roomful of Officer Carlisles studying my picture made me want to crawl away and hide, but there was one more question I had to ask. I cleared my throat, painfully aware that the three adults were staring at me.

"Did any of them – the burglars, I mean – go to Hillside High School?"

Officer Carlisle laughed. At least I thought it was a laugh; it sounded more like a snort.

"Why would you think that?" he asked.

I shrugged, unwilling to admit anything to him.

"No," he said, "it was a professional job. Done by a gang of men in their twenties." He snorted again, like it was the funniest thing he'd heard all day, and shook his head. "Not some little school kids." He said the last bit with a sneer.

Mum might have forgiven Officer Carlisle for being so unhelpful the night of the burglary, but that didn't mean I had to. "I've got homework to do," I said and headed for my room.

I did have homework, but I had no intention of doing it. I had too much to think about. I pulled out my sketchbook and drew a quick caricature of Carlisle snorting, a tiny teacup in his meaty hand. As soon as I was finished, I felt bad about doing it. The man was annoying, but he'd done his job. He'd caught the burglars. I tore the picture out of the book, crumpled it up and threw it in the recycle bin.

The burglars were in jail and I'd finally seen how pathetic Euan really was. I should be free from fear, but I wasn't. I leafed through the sketchbook, stopping at the drawing I'd made after I'd built the golem's body. The picture showed an enormous mud man with a gaping hole for a mouth, rampaging through the woods, destroying everything that got in its way. Once again my mind drifted back to the last story I'd read on the internet. I was beginning to think making a monster had been a really bad idea.

I turned back a couple more pages to the drawing I'd done of the back garden after the burglary. I looked at the jaggedy lines, the garish colours and the lawn, which was a tangled mess of squiggles. I wondered how it would come out if I drew it now? Two round spiky blobs caught my attention. I squinted at them; they looked almost like hedgehogs lying with their little feet in the air. Had the golem killed them because I'd drawn them there? I snapped the sketchbook shut. I was letting my imagination run away with me.

I called Lucy to let her know the burglars had been caught and that we'd even got some of our stuff back. I let her bubble on for a couple of minutes, and then I told her I had to go. It was too difficult to listen to her happy chatter when I was still feeling bad. Now I knew Euan had nothing to do with the break-in, I felt even worse about setting a great big monster after him.

I heard Officer Carlisle leave, so I wandered back out to the living room. Mum was ordering Indian takeaway. I picked up a biscuit and took a bite.

"Why so glum, Mouse?" Mum asked, putting down the phone.

Before I could come up with a good answer, the back door banged open and Dad came down the hall carrying a dead magpie. Its head lolled about sickeningly as he laid it on a sheet of newspaper on the floor.

I stopped chewing. A crumb caught in my throat and I started coughing uncontrollably. Mum handed me something in a cup. I drank it down without tasting it, my eyes fixed on the dead bird. Had the golem killed it too?

"Why are you bringing that in here?" Mum asked, crossing the room.

"I thought your students might want a change from drawing boring old plants," said Dad. "Her neck is broken," he added.

Feeling sick, I dropped the rest of my uneaten biscuit onto the coffee table.

"Poor thing," said Mum, crouching down beside the dead bird and stretching her wing out. Her black feathers turned blue as they caught the light from the lamp. "She must have run into a window."

Dad shook his head. "I found her back by the wall."

Mum frowned. "Magpies are too clever to run into walls. I wonder what got her."

"She's not the first dead animal I've found in the back garden either," said Dad. "Yesterday morning I found a pair of sparrows and a mouse. This morning I found a couple of hedgehogs. Now this. All with their necks broken."

My legs suddenly too weak to hold me up, I sank onto the nearest chair.

"A weasel?" Mum suggested.

Dad shook his head. "Weasels have a bad reputation, but they hunt to eat. Whatever is killing these poor creatures isn't doing it for food."

"A cat then," said Mum.

A cat was no match for a magpie, but I kept my mouth shut. I knew the truth, but my parents would never believe me even if I told them.

Henry started barking frantically next door. My skin grew cold. What if the golem decided to protect the house from him? I couldn't let this go on any longer. It was too late to go tonight – it was already getting dark – but tomorrow morning I'd get up early, go find Michael and force him to put an end to the golem once and for all.

# 17. THE SHED

That night, wind came screaming across the city again. It chased itself around my dreams until I woke into a world howling with its fury. I snapped on the light.

There was a thump outside and a long, low moan, barely audible over the wind. I sat perfectly still, clutching the duvet so tightly my knuckles turned white, waiting for a sound from my parents' room, waiting for them to get up and tell me everything was going to be all right. The wind hurled itself against the house. I heard ash and masonry clatter down the chimney into the living-room fireplace, but my parents' room remained quiet.

Somewhere outside, a door creaked open. Another creak, and then a bang. *Creak, bang. Creak, bang.* Had the boards across the garden door been prised open? Was someone or something sneaking in?

I squeezed my eyes shut, but being blind frightened me more. I had to know what was happening. I opened my eyes and let go of the duvet. Mouth dry, palms damp, I crawled out of bed and tiptoed to the window.

I grabbed the edge of the curtain. I was about to peek

out when I realised my light was still on. Whoever was out there would be able to see in, but I wouldn't be able to see out. I went back around my bed and turned it off. I stood in the dark for a minute, waiting for my eyes to adjust, listening to the door banging outside, feeling my courage leaking slowly away. If only my parents would wake up.

I had a sudden sickening thought. What if Dad did get up and went out to see what was wrong and the golem mistook him for a burglar? I'd created it. I'd seen inside its head. All that rattled around in there was soil, pebbles and a few twigs. So far it had killed a bunch of birds, a mouse and some hedgehogs, none of which had posed a threat. Obviously I couldn't count on it to know the difference between the good guys and the bad.

The one thing Michael had repeated over and over again was that if I did all the work, the golem would recognise me as its master. It would not hurt me. I was the only one who could safely go out there and fix whatever was banging.

I felt my way to the window, pulled the curtain back a couple of centimetres and peered out. All I could see was darkness and dancing shadows. Feeling sick to my stomach, I pulled an old jumper, a pair of tracksuit bottoms and some socks out of my dresser. I didn't bother to take off my pyjamas, just put my clothes on over the top.

I slipped out of my room and crept down the hall to the back door. I needn't have worried. The storm was so loud I could have clomped across the floor in wooden shoes and no one would have heard.

I pulled on my wellies and waterproof jacket, unlocked the door, pocketed the keys, took a deep breath and shoved it open. The wind howled past me, sending leaves skittering down the hall. Using all my strength, I held the door open and edged outside. As soon as I was through, it slammed shut. In case that had woken my parents, I pulled out the keys and locked the door behind me. Fetching another set of keys would slow them down while I dealt with whatever was out here, but it also meant I was on my own. No one would be coming to my rescue.

I turned around slowly, keeping my back pressed against the door. My hair whipped around my face. I thought about the size of the golem, about how thick I'd made its limbs and the club-like hands I'd given it. At the time it had seemed like a good idea, but now I was out here alone in the storm, I wished I'd given it at least one weakness.

I held my hair back and peered into the darkness. Parts of the garden were lit by the streetlamps in front of the house, but most of it was in shadow. What I could see was moving constantly: the grass shifting restlessly, the birch sapling bending up and down, and the bushes around the edges rustling like they were infested with hundreds of rabid rats. Everywhere a swarm of dead leaves swirled and danced. I had made the golem out of earth and leaves and bits of sticks; if it was hiding in the shadows of the garden, I wouldn't be able to tell it apart from anything else.

I thought I could see the cross of boards still nailed over the door in the wall, but I wasn't sure. I knew what was making all the noise, though. The door of Dad's shed had come unlatched and the wind was slamming it against the wall. All I had to do was lock it up again and I could go back to the warmth and safety of my bed.

Hunched against the wind, panting as it blew the breath right out of me, I fought my way into the night. Halfway across the lawn I remembered a movie Lucy and I had stolen from her older brother's room one night. It was about a crazy man with a chainsaw who stalked his victims. To keep ourselves from being completely terrified, we made fun of the people in the movie. They kept doing stupid, dangerous things. Now here I was, on my own, outside in the middle of a storm, my only route of escape locked behind me, and unlike them, I knew there was a monster on the loose.

I staggered towards the shed. The door kept slamming against the wall. Grabbing hold of it, I dragged it shut. I was about to lock it, when I heard a thump inside. Startled, I lost my grip. The wind caught the door and slammed it open again.

"Hello," I called. "Is anyone in there?" Inside was blacker than the blackest pastel in my box.

Another thump.

I stepped inside, reached along the wall and flicked the switch. Nothing happened. A cold finger of fear slid down my spine. Slowly I edged along the wall, leaves swirling around my feet, my eyes straining to see.

*Bang!* The door slammed shut behind me.

I ran over and pounded on it, shouting for help. The wind howled louder, drowning out my voice.

Something rustled behind me. I pushed at the door. It opened a crack. I leaned my shoulder against it and shoved as hard as I could. The door swung open and I tumbled out onto the ground.

I just wanted to lie there and cry but I got up, eyes stinging from the wind and my unshed tears, and pulled the door closed. I tried to lock the padlock but it was jammed. With shaking hands, I turned the knob around the numbered dial a couple of times and tried again. This time the padlock clicked tight.

As I ran to the house, it began to rain. Big drops pelted down on me as I fumbled for my key. I was trembling so much I couldn't fit it into the lock. Behind me, the shed door rattled like something was trying to get free. The key slipped out of my hand and fell into the grass. I dropped to my knees, frantically feeling for it.

A low inhuman wail filled the air. My fingers closed on the key. I scrambled to my feet, unlocked the door and stumbled inside.

Compared to the racket outside, it was peaceful in the house. The rhythmic sound of my father's snores welcomed me home as I locked the door behind me, took off my coat and wellies and snuck back down the hall to my room.

I pulled the curtain open and squinted into the gloom. The rain was coming down harder now but the wind was quieting. Branches and debris lay everywhere, but as far as I could see there were no hulking shadows walking around, no brutish heads peeking over the wall. I could still hear the shed door rattling, but it was gentler now. I'd probably just imagined there was something inside. Still, to be safe, I'd check in the morning daylight, before Dad started his workday.

I fumbled with the alarm clock and tumbled into bed.

Knocking woke me.

"Wake up, Mouse," called my mum in a sing-song voice. She really needed to stop calling me that. I groaned and pulled the duvet up over my head, feeling like I hadn't slept a wink, though my grogginess proved I had.

"This might sound like an odd question," said Mum, coming into the room, "but did you happen to go outside last night?"

Memories of my adventure came rushing in. "No," I said, wide awake now. "Why would you ask that?" I was glad my face was covered. Mum could always tell when I was lying.

"There are leaves all over the hallway," she said.

"The wind must have blown them under the door," I said, feeling sick as I remembered the leaves dancing around my ankles in the shed.

My alarm hadn't woken me! I pulled the duvet off my face. It was after seven o'clock.

"Where's Dad?" I asked, trying to keep the panic out of my voice.

"Out back in his shed," said Mum. "Where else would he be?"

I listened to the silence. "But there's no noise," I said. "Why isn't he making any noise?"

"How should I know? Maybe he's drafting a new project."

Or maybe a giant mud-monster had him pinned to the ground. I sprang out of bed, pushed past Mum and ran down the hall.

"Where are you going?" she called.

"I've got to talk to Dad," I shouted.

"In your pyjamas? It's cold outside."

There was no time to explain. I crammed my bare feet into my boots, grabbed my coat and ran outside. Through the open door of the shed, I could see my father sprawled on the floor.

## 18. THE BULLY

"Dad!" I shouted, dashing towards the shed. "Hold on, I'm coming."

He looked up as I came in. "Ah, good timing, Mouse," he said. "I'm in desperate need of a small pair of hands."

"You're okay?" I asked. "There wasn't anything in here?"

"Of course I'm okay," he said. "Certainly doing better than that poor fellow." He pointed to a blackbird lying dead on the floor. "No mystery this time. I must have locked him in yesterday evening. In his panic to get out he threw himself against the window, knocked himself out and died."

Had the bird still been alive last night? Had I been the one to lock him in? It seemed the more I tried to make things right, the more things went wrong.

"I could really use your help," said Dad. "The storm cut off the electricity to the shed. I've got to run another wire back to the house. I need you to fit your hand down this tube and grab it when I feed it through."

By the time I finished helping Dad, I was filthy and I'd lost twenty minutes of Michael-seeking time. As he spliced the wires together, I brushed as much dirt as

I could off my pyjamas and surveyed the garden. My heart skipped a beat.

There were two tray-sized marks in the bare soil next to the wall. I ran over. They were sunk about ten centimetres deep. The golem must have jumped over the wall and its weight had pressed its feet into the ground when it landed. Had it been in the garden last night when I was out here? I shivered.

"What've you got there, Mouse?" Dad asked, coming up behind me. "That's odd," he said, kneeling down to get a closer look.

How was I going to explain giant footprints to my father?

"We must have moles," he said, getting back to his feet.

"Moles?" I asked. It was about as far from the truth as was possible to go.

"Yes," said Dad. "They tunnel through the earth, weakening the ground, and then all it takes is a bit of disturbance and boom, it caves in."

The marks by the wall didn't look like they'd collapsed from below, they looked like they'd been stomped from above. But I wasn't going to squash Dad's mole theory, not if it would keep him safe from the truth.

"Look!" Dad exclaimed, walking back towards the shed. "Here's some more. See how they follow a line. There must be a tunnel running along under here." Dad was pointing at a couple of wide half-moon holes. I couldn't make sense of them until I thought about sneaking down the hallway. They were exactly the sort of marks a tiptoeing golem might make. I imagined it creeping up behind me as I was trying to shut the shed door. I shivered again. Dad saw me.

"You'd better go get dressed," he said. "Don't worry about the moles."

I went inside, threw on my uniform, tugged my hair into a ponytail, grabbed my sketchbook, shoved it into my backpack and headed for the front door. I had to find Michael and make him get rid of the golem. Having a monster in my back garden did not make me feel safer. It made me feel completely terrified.

"Not so fast, Mouse," said Mum, coming out of the kitchen as I was pulling on my boots. "You didn't eat any breakfast."

"I'm not hungry," I said.

She came down the hall and peered into my face. "You look pale and tired. Are you all right?"

"I'm fine," I said, glancing anxiously at the door. "I just don't want to be late."

Mum checked her watch. "You don't have to leave for another half hour."

"I've got to meet Lucy, we're supposed to prepare something..." I trailed off, my mind too busy imagining golems tiptoeing across the garden to think what Lucy and I might have to prepare.

"At least let me make you some lunch," said Mum.

"But Lucy—"

"Lucy can wait five minutes," she said, bustling back into the kitchen.

Five minutes later, a bag of sandwiches in my hand, I waved to Mum, waited for her to shut the front door and then ran up the road towards the park gate.

It was another cold, grey day and after my close call with the golem, the woods looked even more dark and forbidding than ever. I stood at the gate trying to muster the courage to go through it. I told myself that the fact I'd survived being in the garden with the golem meant the spell had worked. It knew not to hurt me. But then the image of the golem throttling a magpie flashed before my eyes and the little bit of courage I'd pulled together faded away. My shoulders sagged. I couldn't do it. I couldn't go in there. Maybe Michael would finally show up at school today. I turned and walked back down the road, hating myself for being such a coward. I was not Edda the Brave, I was Edda the Mouse. The sooner I stopped pretending otherwise, the safer everyone would be.

Michael wasn't at school when I got there, not that I really expected him to be, but Lucy was. Mr Bradbury glared at me when I came into the library, but I didn't care. Some things are more important than worrying about getting in trouble.

"Great news about the police catching the burglars," whispered Lucy, as I sat across the table from her. "You must be relieved."

"Not really," I said. I told her everything that had happened since I'd talked to her on the phone, from Dad bringing in the dead magpie, to me shutting the shed door in the middle of the storm. I told her about the wailing I'd heard in the night and about the footprints I'd found in the morning.

"I'm sure there's a good explanation," said Lucy. "You

can't really believe there's a monster doing all this?"

Ignoring her question, I took out my sketchbook and opened it to the drawing I'd made of the golem rampaging through the woods. "This is what it looks like," I said. "Or at least this is what I made it to look like. I haven't seen it since it came alive."

"Edda—"

"I know you don't believe me, but please help me anyway." I could feel tears pricking at the corners of my eyes. "Michael's disappeared. I don't have anyone else..."

Mr Bradbury cleared his throat loudly.

"Of course I'll help," she whispered, very quietly. "But you have to promise if I find proof Michael's playing a trick on you, you'll stop acting so crazy."

I nodded. Nothing would make me happier than to be wrong about all of this.

Lucy pulled the sketchbook across the table and studied the picture. "What's on its chest?" she asked.

"Symbols from Michael's book. He wouldn't tell me what they meant, but he said –" I struggled to remember "– he said *abraq ad habra*, which means 'I create with words'. I think it was those letters that did the magic, that made the golem come alive."

"Magic letters?" asked Lucy sceptically. "Well, let's see if we can find them on the computer."

I followed her over to the bank of computers, and she scrolled through the menu of international fonts.

"There, that one," I said, pointing to a series of symbols that looked similar to the ones I'd drawn. They were followed by the word "Hebrew".

"So not magic after all," said Lucy smugly.

"But what do they mean?" I asked.

Lucy found a translation page on the web, but we couldn't figure out how to type in Hebrew letters. I went over to ask Mr Bradbury if there was a Hebrew-English dictionary in the library. He sniffed. "Not on the budget they give me to run this place."

I returned to Lucy. "We'll have to go to the Central Library. Can you come after school?"

"As long as I practise my fiddle for half an hour at home first," she said. "Since my cousin failed his music exam, Mum's been pretty strict."

"Okay," I said. "I'll meet you there."

The bell rang. Lucy had books to check out and I hadn't been to my locker yet, so I left without her. As I walked down the hall, Euan appeared.

I thought about the animals with their necks snapped and the wool I'd given the golem. I had to warn him.

"Hey," I called.

Euan looked up, saw me, turned round and hurried away.

It was strange. When I passed Euan in the cafeteria, sitting with Murdo and George, he made his usual stupid mouse face and laughed, but whenever I saw him by himself, he always seemed to be walking away from me. By the time school ended, I still hadn't managed to warn him.

Lucy rushed off to practise, but instead of heading straight to the Central Library, I hung around the playground wondering what to do. I was angry with Michael for getting me into this mess and then skiving off for days on end. He was probably hiding in his tower, playing with Benedict, waiting for me to come to him. Being the hopeless mouse that I was, I couldn't go to the tower while there was a great big hulking monster lurking in the woods – my great big hulking monster, I corrected myself. I kicked an empty juice carton across the tarmac.

I could at least go find Euan and tell him to stay off the hill. It was the right thing to do. I gave the empty carton one final kick and set off reluctantly in the direction of the big houses where Euan lived.

The closer I got, the slower I walked. I had no idea what to say to Euan. He'd think the golem story was completely mad and it would give him a whole new set of things to stick on my locker. I sighed. If I got lucky, I wouldn't be able to tell which house was his and I'd have to give up. But at least I would have tried.

I'd only passed a couple of houses when I recognised a shiny new mountain bike leaning up against a shiny maroon sports car. The bike belonged to Euan.

I was standing across the street staring at it, trying to come up with something to say, when the front door opened. Without thinking, I jumped behind the nearest hedge. A man came out, young, maybe just a bit older than eighteen. He was about the same height as Euan but even more strongly built, like a rugby player. Just like Euan, his blond hair stood straight up from his heavy, frowning forehead. He saw the bike against the car, stopped in his tracks and shouted Euan's name.

"What?" said Euan, coming around the side of the house.

"Is that your bike?" asked the man menacingly, striding over to the car.

Euan took a couple of steps back. Even from across the road I could see big splotches of red spreading across his face.

"If there's a scratch on my paint job, you're dead," said the man. He picked up the bike and threw it on the tarmac in front of the car. Euan flinched.

The man ran his finger along the car, while Euan cowered against the side of the house.

"You're lucky this time," said the man with a sneer. He opened the car door and jumped inside. "And there's not going to be another." He slammed the door shut and started the engine.

Euan figured out what was going to happen before I did. He jumped in front of the car, waving his arms.

"Dad bought this for me," he yelled. "Next time he phones, I'll tell him what you did."

His brother rolled down the window and leaned out, a fake smile pasted across his thin lips. "It was an accident," he said, gunning the engine. "You're always leaving that bike where it doesn't belong. Sooner or later something bad was bound to happen."

He revved the engine again and Euan leapt out of the way, falling into a holly bush. The car jumped forward, crushing the bicycle under its wheels. Then it peeled down the road, tires squealing, and disappeared around the corner.

Shakily, Euan got to his feet. His jeans were torn at the knee and blood dripped from a large scrape across the side of his hand. He stumbled over to his mangled bike and squatted down. He began to stroke it like it was his pet dog. Even from my hiding place, I could see his bicycle was a complete wreck. He must have thought the same thing because he rocked back on his heels, gazed up at the cloudy sky, and moaned.

I now had a pretty good idea of who had given Euan the black eye, and it wasn't the golem. Maybe I'd been wrong about the whole wool thing. I had wished ill on Euan, though, so I still felt like I owed him something. Besides, watching him get bullied by his horrible brother made me feel sorry for him. Maybe there was some way I could deal with the golem and help Euan all at the same time.

Euan had his back to me and his head down. Slowly, I stood up and stepped out onto the pavement. Edda the Mouse would have been trembling in her shoes, terrified that Euan would give her a pounding once he realised she'd witnessed his humiliation. Edda the Brave remained perfectly calm.

As I walked across the street, Euan got to his feet – still without noticing me – picked up the remains of his bike, and carried it around to the back of his house. I followed.

# 19. FINDING FEAR

Euan had abandoned his bicycle in the middle of the lawn, but at first I couldn't see him anywhere. I was about to go back to the front of the house and ring the bell, when I spotted a huddle of torn and dirty clothes sitting on the patio steps. As I walked towards him, Euan wiped his face on the sleeve of his jacket.

"You're really cruising for a bruising today," he said, but he stayed where he was, hunched up on the damp steps, looking way too miserable to mean it.

I took a deep breath. "I need your help," I said.

Euan stared at me like I'd grown antlers and a tail. "You want me to help you?" I nodded. "Help you do what? Stick your head in a toilet?" he asked. I wasn't scared, not after what I'd seen.

"I need someone big and strong," I said, hoping flattery would get him on my side, "to help me get rid of something on Corstorphine Hill." I had to get him to agree to help before I told him about the golem, otherwise I'd just be giving him something else to call me names about.

"Something or someone?" he asked, his good eye narrowed.

"Kind of both," I replied. "And before I tell you what it is, I need to ask you something." I had to make sure I wouldn't be putting him in any danger. "Have you been mountain biking on the hill in the last couple of days?"

"Are you making fun of me?" he asked, looking down at his mangled bicycle.

"No, of course not," I said hastily. "I just wanted to know if you'd seen anything weird when you were up there."

"Weird, how?" he asked. I hesitated, should I tell him about the golem now? I couldn't see a way round it. If he decided to make fun of me, then maybe I deserved it.

"You know Michael in our class?" I asked.

"The tall annoying kid with the ugly glasses?" he asked.

I nodded. "Well, he..." I hesitated again and then it all came rushing out, "...he got me to make this huge monster out of mud and now its prowling around Corstorphine Hill killing things, birds and small animals, and I'm worried it might do something worse, not that it isn't bad enough already, and I, um, wondered if you might have seen it when you were up there?"

He stared at me like I was an alien again, but at least he wasn't making a rodent-face or shoving me into the wall. "You're completely mental," he said finally.

"So you haven't seen anything?" I asked again.

"No, I haven't and I've been there every day since

Dad sent me the bike." He looked over at it again.

The weight of guilt lifted off me. If the golem was going to hurt him, surely it would have done so by now. "So will you help?" I asked.

"Why would I help you do anything?" he asked. Good question. I could blackmail him. Say I'd tell people I'd seen him crying, but that could backfire really badly.

"I just have a feeling you're the right person to do it," I said, which was true, though I couldn't say why I felt that way, and it sounded silly when I said it out loud.

The words seemed to work though. Euan sat up a little straighter and his face lost some of its sullenness. "So what, you want me to be like your bodyguard, protect you from your imaginary monsters so you don't have to be such a scaredy cat?"

"No," I said, "I want you to help me get rid of it."

"You won't tell anyone, will you?" he asked.

"About you helping me?" I asked, confused.

"Well, yeah, that too, but I meant about the bike," he said. "My dad works in Dubai and my mum goes to stay with him sometimes. A lot of the time it's just me and my brother. It was my fault; I shouldn't have left my bike there."

I didn't think that was true, but I didn't know what to say. "My dad bought me a second-hand bike at a place called the Bike Station," I said. "It's a great bike and it wasn't that expensive."

"Second hand is for losers," he said. Maybe I was wasting my time.

"Are you going to help me or not?" I asked.

"Why not?" he said. "I've got nothing better to do." He scowled at the wreck of his bicycle.

"Great," I said. "But we have to go to the Central Library first, to meet Lucy and figure out what to do."

Euan wouldn't go with me on the bus – he was worried someone would see us together – but he agreed to meet me at the library, since, "No one but complete nerds would be caught dead there anyway."

I opened my sketchbook, feeling like I was stripping myself naked, and set the picture I'd drawn of the golem on the table in front of Lucy and Euan. We were sitting on leather chairs in the lobby under the broad wooden stairs that led up to the Reference Library.

"Whoa, that's one ugly bloke," said Euan appreciatively. Lucy glared at him but he ignored her. "He's much cooler than your mouse girl. You know, you could draw for comics."

"Thanks," I mumbled, embarrassed at the compliment.

"I only saw it before it came alive," I said. "So I had to guess about its expression."

"You do know your friend's completely mental, right?" said Euan to Lucy.

"Why are you here again?" Lucy asked him coldly.

"If we're going to take on an eight-foot-tall mud-monster we need someone on our side who is at least over five feet," I said. Euan smirked and Lucy opened her mouth to protest, but I held up my hand. "I know what you both think, but you have to believe me. The golem exists."

"Have you seen it?" asked Euan.

I shook my head. "But you don't always have to see something to believe in it."

"Edda," said Lucy, "Michael is playing a trick on you. Before you got here, I looked up the word on its chest. It's Hebrew for 'fear.'"

"Cool," said Euan. "Maybe I'll write that on your locker next time." Lucy glared at him. He smirked again.

"Fear?" I repeated, ignoring Euan. I'd been expecting something more mysterious, more alchemical, a riddle maybe, not a simple everyday word.

"I think it's the punchline of his joke," said Lucy. "He wanted you to be afraid and now you're giving him what he wants."

"No," I said, "I asked him to help me get over my fears; it's what the golem was supposed to be for. That's probably why he had me write the word on its chest."

"Or it's like a tag," said Euan. Lucy and I stared at him blankly. "You know," he said, "graffiti. People spray paint these things all over the place like signatures. Tags say 'this belongs to me.'"

"You mean like dogs peeing everywhere," said Lucy, "marking their territory."

"But it's not a tag, is it?" I said irritably. "It's not my name or even Michael's name, it's just a word."

"We're not getting anywhere like this," said Lucy. "Why don't you tell me everything Michael told you to do to make this golem?"

I listed all the things I'd collected and explained how I'd made the creature out of mud, then put in its clay heart. While I talked, Lucy took notes and Euan fidgeted, clearly bored.

"You said recording the roar was your idea," said Lucy. "So why did you choose the lion?"

"Michael said it had to be something ferocious."

"Can you remember his exact words?" Lucy asked, pen poised over her notebook.

I frowned, struggling to remember. "He asked me what animals scared me the most..." I remembered something else: "At the Botanic Garden, he was disappointed when I told him spiders didn't frighten me. He said that the golem wouldn't work if I wasn't frightened."

"And what about when you first met Michael?" Lucy asked. "What were you feeling then?"

"Annoyed," I said, which also summed up how I was feeling about him now. "He came biking up the street the night my house got broken into. He stopped and stared at me like I was a television programme for his entertainment."

"Your house got broken into?" asked Euan. "And you think this monster did it?"

"No, Michael got her to make the golem after the burglary, to protect the house, because she was scared," said Lucy.

I glared at her. "Thanks for spelling that out," I said.

Lucy blushed. "I mean, you'd just found out someone had gone into your house, rummaged through your private things, stolen..." As I continued to glare, she trailed off. "I'd have been scared if it was me."

"I wouldn't have been," said Euan.

"Of course you would have," said Lucy, rounding on him angrily. "You are worse than Michael. All either of you wants to do is make others afraid, because inside you're both terrified."

Lucy was wrong of course. Michael's insides were as hard and cold as an iron fence in winter. Euan was afraid, but for good reasons. "It's not like that," I said.

"Why are you defending them?" Lucy asked me. She turned to Euan. "After what you said to her the next day, Edda even thought you had something to do with the robbery."

"Wait, is that why you were late for school on Wednesday and why you were blubbering to your mummy?" Euan asked. I was tempted to point out that I'd seen him blubbering less than an hour ago. Euan must have remembered the same thing because he looked sheepishly at his shoes. "Look, I'm sorry I called you a cry-baby, I didn't know you'd been robbed."

"Not the cry-baby bit, what you said after," said Lucy. "When you asked if she was afraid of the dark."

I'd forgotten about that. I looked at Euan, hoping he had a good explanation. He appeared genuinely confused. "I don't know what you're talking about," he said.

"Don't you?" said Lucy, in her I-don't-believe-you-for-a-moment voice.

Thinking back, there was something not quite right about that whole incident. I'd heard what I thought was Euan's voice, but when I'd turned around I couldn't see him anywhere – Euan never faded into the background

– and when I'd bolted for the toilets seconds later, I'd run straight into Michael.

"Euan didn't ask me if I was afraid of the dark," I said, putting it all together. "Michael did."

"What?" said Lucy, taken aback.

Everything Michael had done, everything he'd got me to do had been aimed at scaring me: building up my fear of Euan, almost getting us caught, daring me into the lion's cage.

"It all makes perfect sense now," I said excitedly. "Lucy, you were right, Michael wanted me to be afraid, not because he's a bully," I glanced at Euan, "but because fear feeds the golem. I think he wanted to make the golem all along, and he needed me and my fear to do it." So much for being my friend.

"He is a little creep," said Euan.

"So you believe in Edda's monster now?" asked Lucy.

"No," said Euan, "but I believe Michael gets off on scaring people."

I remembered the scene between them in the hallway. "He frightened you too," I said. "What did he say?"

"He didn't say anything," said Euan, turning beetroot red and staring at his feet, "and he doesn't scare me."

Lucy gave him a scornful look. "It keeps coming back to Michael," she said to me. "What do we know about him?"

"He started school the day after the break-in," I said.

"I bet he's your burglar," said Euan.

"The police caught the burglars," said Lucy, "and they weren't thirteen-year-old boys with glasses."

"He's got a room in the old tower on top of

Corstorphine Hill," I said, "with all kinds of crazy books and things in it. He idolises the guy he's named after. I looked him up on the internet. *The* Michael Scot was born at the end of the 1100s. He spoke lots of languages, translated books – some with really weird titles. He worked for an emperor doing astrology mostly, and there were some strange stories about him having dinner parties with food that spirits stole from kitchens in other countries. That's about it."

"Except most of it's not about our Michael, is it?" Lucy said. "It's about the Michael Scot who died eight hundred years ago."

"Actually, there's no record of the other Michael Scot being dead," I said. "No grave, no body."

"So now you're saying the creepy kid is some eight-hundred-year-old wizard?" asked Euan. "Mental," he mouthed.

"Not a wizard, an alchemist," I corrected. "And no, I'm not saying that, though he probably owns all the books the other Michael translated. I'm just saying he knows how to do some really bizarre things."

"Like the girl said, it all comes back to Michael," said Euan. "Let's go to this tower and make him admit he's just a sad idiot with no friends who gets off on scaring gullible, mousey little girls."

I glared at him.

"I agree," said Lucy. "We should go have a word with Michael." She looked at her watch. "But I can't go now, my parents expect me home for tea in half an hour."

I checked my watch, so did my folks, but I couldn't stand to spend another night like the last one. If I could just talk to Michael, maybe I could convince him to stop the golem.

"We could meet up after," I said. "You could say you were coming to mine to do homework and I'll tell my parents I'm going to yours."

"It'll be dark by then," said Lucy. "Why don't we just wait until tomorrow after school?"

"You've got fiddle lessons tomorrow," I said. "Besides, it won't take long. The tower is only a wee bit in. If Michael admits the whole thing was a hoax, then we can all go home and I'll get to sleep tonight. Otherwise..."

"What's Euan going to tell his parents?" asked Lucy, seeming to like the idea of him joining us more now that we were going into the woods after dark.

Euan shrugged. "My brother doesn't care," he said. "I can do what I like."

## 20. THE HUNT

After dinner, I asked Dad if I could go to Lucy's to finish my homework. He said fine, as long as I was home by nine. Since it was only just six, that wouldn't be a problem. I promised to be back in time.

I was the first to arrive at the park gate. The sky was already beginning to darken and shadows lay thick under the trees. I wanted to stay in the brightness of the nearby streetlamp, but I was worried one of my parents might come out and see me waiting there, so I opened the gate, steeled my nerves and slipped behind the wall. What had seemed like a good idea when we were all snug and warm inside the library, now seemed completely mad. The golem was out there, I'd built it, I'd seen its huge footprints and the creatures it had killed. So why had I suggested heading into the woods in the dark, where it was probably lurking? I could feel my courage leaking down through my hollow belly and out my cowardly toes. I probably would have run back home with my tail between my legs like Henry, if Lucy hadn't turned up just then.

"Edda, are you there?" she whispered at the gate.

When I came out of the shadows she actually jumped. We looked at each other and started to giggle. I felt better immediately.

Euan arrived a couple of minutes later, a bulging rucksack on his back and a camera slung around his neck.

"We're just going to the tower to talk to Michael, right?" asked Lucy, eyeing his bag.

Euan shrugged. "Dad bought me loads of camping stuff last summer. He was going to take me to the Highlands. I thought some of it might be useful." He dug around in his rucksack. Thinking about Euan in that big house with just his bully of a brother for company, I found myself feeling sorry for him again. He pulled out a light on a strap, which he tied around his head. "I brought these in case it gets too dark." He handed Lucy and I shiny new torches.

"The tower's only ten minutes away," I said, "and the path's easy to follow."

"Like those boy scouts say: be prepared," said Euan.

"And the camera?" I asked, wondering if he'd changed his mind about the golem.

He shrugged again and grinned. "Just in case."

I led the way up the darkening path, getting more and more nervous the further we went. All I could hear was our footsteps. The rest of the world was completely still and silent, like it was holding its breath, waiting for something terrible to happen.

Euan broke the silence, whistling a tune from a car commercial. It made me uncomfortable. He was letting everyone and everything know exactly where we were.

"Shh," I hissed, smacking him on the arm. "It'll hear us."

"Is widdle Edda scared of the dark?" he asked in an imitation of Michael's voice. I scowled at him. "What?" he said. "It's not like there's a big scary monster waiting out there or anything."

"Just keep quiet, okay?" I said.

The ten-minute walk seemed to take twice as long as normal, but finally the tower came into view, the top of it lost in a fog I hadn't seen from the road. A figure stood next to the tower door, too skinny to be the golem.

As we approached, Euan dropped behind. I wondered again what Michael had said to him.

"I've been expecting you for some time now," said Michael.

"Where have you been?" I asked him.

"Exactly where I've always been," he replied.

"You weren't at school," I said.

"Wasn't I?" he said airily. "It must have slipped my mind. Now, did you want something specific or did you just stop by to accuse me of truancy?"

"We came so you could admit you've been playing a trick on Edda," said Lucy.

"Did you?" asked Michael. "Is that why Edda came? Does she think the golem is just a trick?"

Lucy opened her mouth to say something else. "No," I said quickly. "I know the golem is real."

"Yes," said Michael, staring at me unblinking. "I believe you do. You haven't seen it... not yet... but you can feel its pull on you, feel it grow stronger every time you jump at nothing more than your own shadow."

"I want you to stop the golem," I said. "It's been killing innocent creatures."

"Innocent creatures?!" exclaimed Michael. "The hedgehogs have been stealing grass from your garden for months. The mouse was lining her nest with sawdust from your father's shed. As for the sparrows, they have been spying through your window, watching you draw and I know how uncomfortable you are with drawing in public. Do you know what the magpie was doing when the golem caught her? She had just plucked a piece of aluminum foil out of your recycling bin. The golem was merely protecting your house and property. Isn't that what you wanted?"

"No," I said, more loudly than I meant to. Startled, a flock of pigeons rose noisily from the treetops. "That's not... I just wanted everything to go back to the way it was before," I said more quietly, "when I wasn't scared."

"Tell me, Edda, when was that, exactly?" sneered Michael. "Was everything in your little world fine before the big bad burglars walked all over your fuzzy pink sweater?"

I hated him. Euan and Lucy were right; he had never been my friend. He'd done all of this for his own twisted reasons. But what he'd done wasn't just a trick; it was a nightmare.

"No, I didn't think so," continued Michael in a sinisterly soft voice. "You were frightened long before the thieves arrived. That's why you stole a piece of that boy's jumper and placed it deep down inside the golem's stomach where it keeps all its bile and anger. Tell the boy what was in your heart when you did that."

I could feel Euan's gaze hot on my back. My face flushed with shame.

"You got me to do that," I said. "You're the one who showed me the piece of wool by the garden door. You pretended to be Euan when you asked if I was afraid of the dark."

"That piece of wool could have come from anyone, even you or me," said Michael. "But your mind went right to the boy, because you were already afraid of him. I may have suggested making the golem, but you're the one who sculpted a monster to hurt and maim. Your feelings feed its leaden heart."

"Look, you've made your point. I made a mistake. I made loads of mistakes. Everything is miles worse now. I promise next time I'm scared I won't make a monster. Please, just help me make things better," I pleaded.

"That's what I'm trying to do," said Michael, his eyes flashing with annoyance. He suddenly seemed much taller than before and older, though physically he didn't change at all. I blinked. "Do you remember what you wished for?" asked Michael. "The exact words you used?"

I had to think for a moment. "I wished I wasn't afraid all the time," I whispered.

"And are you afraid all the time?" he asked. "Are you afraid now?"

"No, but no one is really afraid all the time." I suddenly remembered what Michael had said about being careful to say exactly the right words. "Hey, you did trick me!" I said.

"Did I?" he asked. "Is that what you really think of me? I'm hurt." He didn't look hurt. He had a smug little smile on his face.

"Please," I said again, "I made a mistake. As long as the golem's out there, the woods aren't safe."

"As long as there are burglars, my house isn't safe," said Michael, in a high voice that sounded nothing like mine. "As long as the golem's out there, we're not safe... Aren't you listening to anything I'm saying? I colluded in your first mistake; I'm not going to help you make another."

"If you knew making the golem was the wrong thing to do, why did you show me how to do it?" I asked.

"I never said it was the wrong thing to do." His smile was almost kindly. "Alchemy is much more complicated than what passes for science in this century. Sometimes it takes more lead than you can imagine to create a single piece of gold. Sometimes you don't get any gold at all."

He turned to go.

"Please," I called after him, "if you won't tell us what to do, at least give us a hint."

"You already know everything you need to know," said Michael. "I'm sorry, I've done what I can for you. My hands are tied in this."

"But you're my friend," I said.

"No," he said, shaking his head sadly, "I'm just the alchemist." Before I could plead again, he slipped inside the tower and shut the heavy iron door. I stared at it in despair, as the deadbolt clicked shut. Lucy and Euan didn't believe the golem existed, and even though Michael knew I was telling the truth he'd just abandoned me. I wanted to pound on the door again, but there was no point. I knew he wouldn't answer.

"Well, that answers my questions," said Euan. "He had me going the first time I met him, when he seemed to know all about my brother, but after listening to him blethering on about turning lead into gold and granting Edda's three wishes by creating a monster, I now know he's just completely mental. Kinda sad, cos he's obviously brainy. Just goes to show what happens when you read too many books."

"Can we go back now?" asked Lucy. "It's getting really dark."

I looked around in surprise. I'd been so focused on trying to get Michael to help, I hadn't noticed the sun setting.

"Don't tell me you believe all this golem rubbish now," said Euan.

"No," said Lucy. "But there could be older kids out here drinking and stuff. I've seen where they set fires."

"Don't worry," said Euan. "According to Edda, you're with one of those scary people right now."

"About that..." I began.

"No worries," said Euan, cutting me off. "It's not like there really is a monster out there waiting to hunt me down, and I guess I kind of deserve it – you being mad at me, I mean, not the being hunted part." He laughed.

I didn't feel any better about what I'd done. I turned to go back down the path to the gate, but Euan snapped his headlamp on and pointed it in the other direction. "Come on," he said. "This is kinda fun. How often do you get to explore a park after dark? Let's go see Edda's golem hole and the footprints. They're close by, right?"

I stared at him. Was he serious? I couldn't see his face because the light strapped to his forehead was blindingly bright.

"Come on, Lucy. You want to help Edda, don't you?" Euan said. I could tell from Lucy's expression that she thought he was completely mad, but Euan didn't seem to notice. "It'll only take a couple of minutes and we might find more evidence that Michael is a fruitcake." The light swung over to my face. "Edda, face your fears, right?"

The thought of going deeper into the woods filled my stomach with quaking ice cubes, but there was a chance that if Euan saw the evidence, he'd finally believe me. Maybe Lucy would too; the dark always made things seem more possible.

"Okay," I said, turning on my torch. "Follow me."

It seemed beyond foolish to go plunging into the thick undergrowth when there was a monster on the loose, so I led them around by the path towards the place Lucy and I had last seen the footprints.

By the time we got there, it was too dark to see much at all. I had to search the ground with my torch for ten minutes before I found one.

Euan looked at it doubtfully. "It doesn't look like much," he said.

"I didn't give the golem any toes," I replied. "Or shoes. But look how the print is deeper at the heel, just like ours are, and there's more of them." I shone the torchlight back, revealing another. "They're all the same distance apart."

Euan took out his camera and pointed it at the prints. His flash went off. All I could see was a big white blotch. I blinked my eyes, but it didn't help.

"You're a complete numpty," I said to the vague blob standing where the flash had come from. "Now none of us can see a thing."

"We need proof it's a trick," he said.

I scowled in his general direction. "I told you, it's not a tri—"

"Shh!" hissed Lucy, grabbing my arm.

I heard it too, a strange fluttering noise, like a thousand leaves suddenly being tossed in the air.

"It's just the wind," I whispered.

"I don't feel a breeze, do you?" asked Lucy.

It was true; the air was completely still.

"But that can't be the golem," I whispered. "Last night, when I heard it coming –" Euan made a dismissive snorting noise. I ignored him. "– it sounded like someone beating the ground like a drum."

*Thump. Thump. Thump.* Cold fear trickled down my back.

"You mean like that?" asked Lucy shakily.

"Yeah," I said, my voice coming out in a strangled squeak.

"Just road crews fixing the tarmac," whispered Euan. "They do it at night when there's less traffic."

The thumping continued, but it grew quieter. The golem was moving away from us. I felt a moment of relief before I realised where it was heading: my house!

"We have to follow it," I said. I had to see for myself what it did out there in the dark while I was sleeping.

"No way," said Lucy. "It's nocturnal. We aren't. We need to get out of here. Go home where it's safe and wait until tomorrow. Then we can come back and track it in the daylight, when we can see what we're doing."

I thought I'd feel triumphant when she finally started believing me, but standing in the dark and hearing the fear in her voice actually made me feel more scared.

"So you believe in the golem now?" asked Euan.

"I believe there's something big out there," she said, her voice wavering.

"Girls," Euan said with a snort, as if the word was an insult, "it's just trees bashing together. If I knew my way in the dark, I'd show you."

"I know my way around," I said. Michael had told me I could stop the golem. Until I did, no one was safe. I had to confront it, but I needed to know more about it first, and I didn't want to go spying by myself. "I could take you there. Unless you're too scared," I added to Euan.

Lucy and Euan followed me back up the path to the tower, which looked dark and deserted now, a blacker shadow against the night sky. Was Michael hiding in there, gloating over the monster he'd made me create, waiting for it to turn on its maker like the golem in that fairy tale had?

"Okay," I whispered. "We can get to the wall behind my house by taking a shortcut through the woods, but we have to be careful because there are brambles and a well, and we have to turn our lights off so it won't see us coming."

"I don't know about this," said Lucy, for about the hundredth time.

"We're just going to see what it's doing," I said.

"It might not even be there," added Euan.

I'd only taken the shortcut once before, but my feet seemed to know the way by themselves. The clouds had drifted apart and the moon was out. It lit our way but it also cast strangely angled shadows everywhere. We walked slowly and in silence as I led them through the undergrowth, around bramble bushes and across clearings. By the time I spotted the familiar clump of birch trees, I felt like we'd been walking all night. I risked whispering to the others to go slowly and be careful.

As we came around the trees, their bark glowing ghostly in the moonlight, we saw the well: a gaping hole, like a mouth in the earth, its rotted wooden safety railing hanging uselessly from its posts. Lucy looked at me, her eyes big black saucers. If I hadn't known it was there, if the moon had stayed hidden behind the clouds, we might not have seen the well until it was too late.

We gave the weak ground around the hole a wide berth, walked on a few more minutes, and finally came to the trail behind the wall. As we walked up it, I started to worry about how easy we were to see. If the golem was guarding my house, then it would be watching the trails. The moonlight was so bright we were casting shadows. How could it not see us? I wanted to get under cover of the trees again, but this section of the trail was lined with thick, knotted patches of brambles. I stopped suddenly, spotting a bramble bush that had been trampled nearly flat. I looked at my friends, pointed at it and pressed my finger to my lips. They nodded wide-eyed, Lucy's face as pale as birch bark. The golem was around here somewhere.

I started walking again. A twig snapped under my foot, as loud as TV gunfire. We all froze. My heart pounded frantically in my chest like it was trying to escape. The only other sound I could hear was the rasping of our breathing. If the golem was nearby, it was staying perfectly still.

Up ahead loomed the huge beech tree that grew behind my house. Its bark looked even more like elephant skin in the moonlight. The sight made me feel a little better, like meeting a good friend when you really need one. The tree had watched over me for a year now; it would do its best to look out for me now. I crept towards it, cringing as my trainers crunched loudly on dry leaves. I hoped the golem's ears were plugged with mud.

I reached the beech and pressed my face gratefully against its trunk. Seconds later Lucy and Euan joined me. We looked at each other, made a silent agreement, and then edged around the trunk until we could see the clearing.

I let out a long slow breath of relief. The clearing was empty. Just the long grass, a couple of boulders and the jagged remains of a large, dead tree. Maybe Euan was right; maybe it was all in my head.

One of the branches on the dead tree started to move, even though there was no wind, pivoting upwards like a giant arm. The golem's colossal head turned towards us. I caught a glimpse of its eyes, two pits I'd poked into its head with a stick, and its wide crater of a mouth, open just like in my drawing. It raised its head, sniffing the air, and rubbed its belly with a hand that had somehow grown fingers and a thumb. *All the better to break necks with*, I thought to myself.

"Run!" we all yelled at the same time.

We ran down the hill, careening around bushes and trees, following the wall away from the hideous monster.

For a moment I thought we were going to get away, but then the terrible thumping started again, faster than before. *Thump-thump, thump-thump, thump-thump.*

"We have to split up," shouted Euan, "or he'll get all of us!" He veered off, tearing through the brambles, into the woods.

The thump-thumping paused. Lucy and I kept running.

"Hey, Golem," we heard Euan shout, "I'm over here!"

The heavy footsteps started again, but this time I could also hear trees groaning, smashing together as the golem, invisible behind us, crashed into the woods, heading after Euan.

"No!" I shouted, stopping in my tracks. I hadn't asked Michael if the wool put Euan in danger. What if I was wrong about him being safe? What if I'd given Euan a death sentence? "Leave him alone!" I screamed at the top of my lungs.

The golem kept thumping after Euan. Lucy came running back towards me.

"Keep going," I whispered to her urgently. She shook her head. "Michael told me it wouldn't hurt me. I'm the only one who can stop it from hurting Euan." I had to hope it was true. "You need to save yourself."

Lucy shook her head again. "The well," she said. "Get it to the well."

It took me a second to figure out what she meant, but when I understood I was impressed. "You are the smartest person in the whole world, you know that?" She gave me a weak smile.

I thought fast. If we called to Euan to lead the golem to the well, it might figure out what we were planning. I had to get it to come after me.

"Golem!" I yelled. "To me!"

The thump-thumping paused. An anguished roar rang through the dark woods, ending in a low moaning wail.

I shivered; it was the same sound I'd heard outside my house last night.

"I think you've confused it," said Lucy. "Try again."

"Golem, as your maker I command you to come to me," I shouted, my voice loud and strong.

It roared again and then started thumping our way.

"I did it," I said happily. "I got it to come after us." I realised what I'd just said, and my excitement drained away. "Run!" I shouted.

# 21. THE PLAN

The thumps moved towards Lucy and me slowly, as if the golem was tired or still confused, but its strides were probably twice as long as ours. We had to get to the well before it did, so we took the trail back up the hill at a run and turned into the woods. We were almost there when Euan crashed through the bushes next to us. He stopped when he saw us and leaned against a tree, panting.

"What're you doing?" he asked between breaths. "I was drawing it away from you... I can take the golem."

"No you can't," said Lucy. "No one can."

The thumps started getting louder and closer together.

"Lucy has a plan," I said. "But we have to get to the well first."

We didn't stop running until we got there, making sure the well lay between the golem and us. The thumps were so loud now, I was expecting to see the golem any second.

"I'll get its attention," I said. "Euan, you be your usual annoying self. Call it names or something. It has to come towards us without looking down."

"And me?" asked Lucy.

"Get ready to run if it goes wrong." I took a deep breath and shouted as loud as I could, "Golem, as your maker I command you to come here as quickly as possible."

The thumps faltered and stopped. I'd confused it again.

"Now, Golem, now," I yelled urgently, worried the plan was going to fail. I nudged Euan. He stepped closer to the edge of the well.

"Come and get me, you stupid mousey cry-baby," he yelled, glancing back at me with a shrug. Lucy was right; he made a pathetic bully. I didn't know why I'd ever been afraid of him.

The thumps started again, but slowly. I started to panic. If the golem emerged from the woods at a walk, it would see the hole.

"You've got to be meaner," I said to Euan, desperately trying to think of a way to inspire him. "Pretend to be your brother."

He turned back towards the woods. "Can't you do anything right, you sorry excuse for a toe-rag?" he yelled.

*Thump-thump. Thump-thump.*

"Be quiet or scram. No one wants you around here!" he shouted, his hands balled into fists.

*Thump-thump-thump. Thump-thump-thump.*

"If you touch my stereo one more time, I'm going to beat you to a pulp. Do you understand? Or do I need to come over there and make you understand?" I could see Euan's back shaking.

The golem broke through the undergrowth and charged towards us.

"Why do you think Mum and Dad left, for some lousy job in the stinking desert? Of course not. They left because they couldn't stand your snivelling, snotty little face. Don't you get it? They went because they hate you. Everybody hates you. It would have been better if you'd never been born."

The golem lunged at him. Lucy screamed. The soil beneath its foot gave way and it plunged into the well, a look of horror on its twisted face. The ground shook as it hit the bottom of the hole.

Lucy and I jumped back but Euan stood frozen in place. A fissure opened in the ground, snaking towards him. A chunk of earth broke off and fell into the widening hole.

"Euan!" I shouted, rushing forward and grabbing his arm as another clump of dirt fell away. "Come on."

He shook his head and blinked, seeming to notice where he was for the first time. We scrambled backwards just as the place where he'd been standing disappeared. Euan pulled his arm out of my grip and staggered away. In the sudden quiet, I heard him retching into the bushes behind us.

"Do you think it's dead?" whispered Lucy.

A high, strangled wailing filled the air. Down at the bottom of that deep, dark hole the golem whimpered. My heart suddenly hurt for the poor, frightened creature. What had we done?

"We have to go," said Euan, returning to my side. "It's big and it's strong. The well won't hold it for long."

He jogged towards the wall, Lucy and I close behind him. None of us spoke, but we were all thinking the same thing: we'd had a narrow escape.

"Wait," I called, as Euan and Lucy passed the big beech tree and kept going. "It'll be faster to climb over."

I slipped in between the wall and the tree and started shimmying up the way Michael had shown me. Euan and Lucy ran back towards me. Euan bent over so Lucy could stand on his back. She pulled herself onto the top of the wall at the same time as I did. As Euan tried to scramble up after us, the golem's wailing cut through the night again.

"Go up the way I did," I whispered urgently. "Put your back against the wall and then walk up the tree trunk."

It took Euan three tries, but finally he made it.

"Look, thanks," he said, squatting next to me on top of the wall, "for calling the golem off. You didn't have to do that."

"Yes, I did," I said, thinking about his horrible brother, his parents who seemed to think buying him stuff made up for not being around, the wool I'd pulled off his jumper and all the stupid things I'd done since the break-in.

"One... two... three," Lucy counted. The three of us jumped into my garden together, landing in a heap on the lawn.

"Are we safe here?" whispered Lucy, as we got to our feet.

"No, it's been in the garden before," I said. "But I don't think it'll come into the house so long as I'm in it

– it's meant to protect me. And it can't leave the hill, so you two will be completely fine once you get home."

Lucy looked at me wide-eyed. "You should sleep at my house tonight," she said, "just in case it's mad at you too now."

"I can't leave my parents."

"Bring them along," said Lucy.

"How would I get them to come?" I asked. "Besides, I did this because I wanted to stay living here. Going to your house would be like giving up."

Lucy opened her mouth to say something more, but at that moment the back light of the house snapped on. A second later Dad appeared in the doorway.

"Mouse, it's you," he said. "I wondered what all the ruckus was. I thought you were at... Oh, hello, Lucy, you're here too." He caught sight of Euan. "Who's this and what does he have on his head?" I looked over at Euan, who was still wearing his headlamp.

"Dad," I said, "this is Euan. We're all lab partners and we're working on a science project." I was too tired and my mind was too full of monsters to come up with anything better, but Dad didn't seem to notice.

"Aren't you going to invite your friends inside?" he asked. "I'm sure your mother can scrounge up some drinks and a packet of Hobnobs."

"That's okay, Dad," I said. "They need to get home."

Lucy looked ready to bolt, but Euan strode towards the door. "I don't know about you two, but working on science stuff has made me really hungry. I feel like I've just run ten miles. I'd love a Hobnob, thanks, Mr Macdonald."

"If we get close enough, maybe we can wipe off the word on its chest and write something else," said Lucy.

We were camped out in my bedroom with a pack of Hobnobs and three glasses of milk. If Mum was surprised that the inseparable pair of Lucy and I had become an inseparable trio, she hadn't said anything.

"Yeah, that's a great idea. We'll just walk up to the big friendly 'fear' monster, rub out its name tag and christen it 'peace and love' with a nice sharp stick," said Euan, helping himself to another biscuit. "It's not that easy to stop a bully."

"You should know," said Lucy.

I elbowed her and she turned deep red, realising what she'd just said. None of us had mentioned the things Euan had shouted at the golem.

"I just meant, the way you used to treat Edda—" I elbowed her harder this time.

"Another Hobnob?" I asked Euan, holding up the packet.

"Lucy's right," said Euan. "I was really horrible to you."

"No worries," I said. "Really. You've more than made up for it." I paused, and told myself to be Edda the Brave. Blushing with shame, I launched into the apology I'd attempted earlier. "I'm sorry I pulled a thread off your jumper and fed it to a mud-monster, hoping it would track you down and beat you up."

Euan stared at me. I thought he was going to yell at me, but instead his face crinkled up and he made a strange kind of snortling noise. It took me a second to recognise what it was: a chuckle.

"Fed it to a mud-monster..." he repeated between snorts, tears leaking out of the corners of his eyes.

Lucy and I looked at each other, astonished, and then we started to giggle too. Lucy laughed so hard, Hobnob crumbs came flying out of her mouth, which made Euan and I laugh even more.

"Hey, what do you feel now?" asked Lucy after the giggle fit had passed and we were all lying on the floor, panting for breath.

"What do you mean?" I said. "Nothing's changed. There's still a monster out there, probably angrier than ever, now that we've trapped it in a hole. We still don't know how to stop it."

"Exactly," said Lucy, her eyes sparkling. "Even though nothing we're facing has changed, one minute it filled us with dread and the next moment we couldn't stop laughing. While I was laughing I wasn't afraid, were you?"

Euan shook his head and reached for another Hobnob.

"And laughter is a sound, a vibration," Lucy continued. "It must carry one of those essence things, right?"

"Like the lion's roar," I said, finally seeing what she was getting at. "It was the roar that made the golem ferocious enough. So if we give it another sound, something that's the opposite of a roar, the two sounds might cancel each other out. Like in science class with the water tank. When the same-sized waves met everything went calm." I grinned at Lucy. She grinned back.

Euan looked from one of us to the other. "If you

think laughing is going to stop the golem, you really are mental," he said. "Besides, it's going to be difficult to laugh when we're running for our lives."

"It doesn't need to be laughter," I said. "It could be any happy sound. Singing..."

"No way," said Euan. "We're not singing to it."

"Or an instrument," I said, getting excited. "Lucy, you could play something happy on your fiddle."

"Yeah, I guess," she said doubtfully. "But shouldn't you be doing it. It's your golem."

I thought about everything I'd learned since I asked Michael to help me get rid of my fears. "I think you can make monsters on your own, but you need your friends' help to stop them. I never would have thought of the well on my own," I said to Lucy. "And we couldn't have trapped the golem in there without your help," I said to Euan. "I can't do this by myself."

"Of course we'll help," said Lucy. "I just meant, maybe it should be you who makes the music."

"No," I said, "you're the music girl. There's something else I'm meant to do." And I knew exactly what it was. "Michael said I should never draw a picture of the golem sitting in a meadow, petting rabbits."

"Why, because it might decide to go rip the heads off fuzzy bunnies?" asked Euan, grabbing another biscuit.

"Don't be so disgusting," I said. "No, because the golem is tied to me and my feelings. Thinking about the golem in the sun surrounded by happy bunnies makes it seem less scary, makes it seem silly. That's why he didn't want me to draw it that way."

"Okay," said Euan, "so far your cunning plan is for

Lucy to play it a jig while you paint a silly picture. What am I going to do, read it sissy poetry?"

"You're going to do what you suggested," I said, the plan forming itself in my head. "While Lucy is playing, keeping it calm and distracted, you'll erase the letters on its chest and put something else there, something that's the opposite of fear."

"You want me to write 'love and peace' on the monster?" said Euan, staring at me as if I'd completely lost my mind.

"Not exactly," I said. "I gave the golem a heart of clay, full of spiky cactus spines, cobwebs and plant guts. You're going to give it a new one. You'll draw a heart in its dirt skin."

"Yeah, cos drawing a soppy Valentine's heart is so much better than poetry," he said. "No way. You do it."

"It's got to be you," I said. "When you call someone names, those names stick to them. Besides, you're the only one tall enough to reach its chest."

Euan shook his head. "Uh-uh. You're forgetting the whole bit where you told it to hurt me. I'm not going anywhere near that thing."

"I thought you said you could 'take it,'" said Lucy.

"Yeah, well I only said that so you two would scram," he replied.

"You'll be fine," I said, hoping I was right. "The golem is tied to me and I don't want it to hurt you any more."

"I'm not sure it got the message," said Euan. "I don't know if you noticed, but it tried to rip my throat out back there."

"That's because you were antagonising it," said Lucy.

"Edda told me to."

"Yeah, and my plan worked, didn't it? This one's going to work too."

Lucy and Euan didn't look convinced.

"Don't you want me to tell you how I know?" I asked.

Neither of them said anything.

"Because I'm not afraid any more."

More silence.

"Do either of you have a better idea?"

"I still think we should sneak up on it while it's asleep and bash its head in," said Euan.

I thought about its pitiful wailing. "No," I said.

"Okay," said Lucy. "We'll try it your way, but not tonight. We should wait until daylight. You said we'd all be safe in our houses, right? Besides, if we're lucky, it'll stay trapped in the well."

"Let's do it first thing in the morning," said Euan. "Skive off school."

"No," said Lucy and I in unison.

"You're going to put more cute little animals' lives at risk just so you don't miss school?" he asked.

"It doesn't seem to do much in the day," I said.

"And I have fiddle lessons after school," said Lucy.

"I don't think you two are taking this monster seriously," said Euan.

For some reason that struck Lucy and I as hilarious. We collapsed into another heap of giggles.

"This is exactly why girls shouldn't fight monsters," said Euan with disgust.

\*

Once the others had left and I was lying alone in bed, in the dark, my confidence started to fade. The whole idea that the three of us could defeat a massive mud-monster seemed crazy.

The wind started up outside, moaning and rustling through the trees. At least I hoped it was the wind. Had the golem escaped? Was I really safe in my bed? I switched the light back on.

"I am Edda the Brave," I repeated to myself, over and over again, until at last I fell asleep.

## 22. LEAD INTO GOLD

The next day, I couldn't focus on my lessons; my mind was too busy going over what we had to do after school. I'd told my friends that it would work, but I wasn't really so sure. I could be putting them in a lot of danger just to fix a mistake that I'd made on my own. Even Lucy seemed distracted. Mrs Philpotts asked her a question, and she just stared at the board blankly.

I kept doodling in the margins of my notebook, trying to figure out how to make the golem appear friendly and happy, but the more I drew, the more everything including the bunnies started to look sinister. As the day ticked by, the butterflies in my stomach turned into hopping frogs.

A shadow fell over my notebook. I covered the page with my arm and looked up, but it was only Euan. He looked around. No one was watching us, so he smiled. "Meet you after school," he whispered, before returning to his desk.

I stared at the pointy-toothed rabbit I'd just drawn. Maybe I should build a dirt rabbit big enough to eat the golem. I hastily scribbled out my drawing.

After school, Lucy rushed off to her lesson, promising to come to my house when she was done. Euan was nowhere to be seen though Murdo and George were kicking a football against the wall. Maybe he'd chickened out. It was probably the sensible thing to do.

With a sigh I trudged down the road. I hesitated at the bottom of Hillside Drive. With one more step I'd be on Corstorphine Hill. The idea of meeting the golem on my own frightened me. Maybe if I skipped...

I'd only gone a few feet when a piece of shadow detached itself from a tall hedge across the road. I froze, heart pounding.

"What are you doing?" asked Euan, coming towards me.

"You told me you'd meet me after lessons," I said angrily to hide my embarrassment.

"That's what I'm doing," he said. "I just didn't want to wait for you at school..."

Typical, he didn't want Murdo and George to see him talking to the Wee Mousie.

"I was skipping," I said, "to see if it made me feel less scared."

"Did it work?" he asked.

I shook my head. "Not really."

I took out my pastels and my sketchbook and sat down at my desk. Knowing this picture would matter, that making it might actually change things in the world, made it that much more daunting. Having Euan hovering behind me didn't help.

"Why don't you go find something to write on the golem with?" I suggested.

"That's okay," said Euan. "I'll just pick up a stick in the park."

"I made it out of mud," I said, "but you heard it thumping around; its flesh must have hardened. You're probably going to need something stronger than a stick."

"Like what?"

"I don't know." All I really wanted was for Euan to leave me alone so I could draw. "Why don't you borrow one of my dad's tools? He's in the shed in the garden."

"What'll I tell him?" Euan asked.

"Just make something up," I said in exasperation.

He finally left and I opened my sketchbook. The two halves of the leaflet for the National Gallery competition fluttered to the floor. Faced with the task of drawing a picture good enough to change a monster into a harmless bunny-lover, it seemed silly to be afraid of making a picture for a contest. I picked up the pieces of leaflet and laid them on the corner of my desk. I closed my eyes and took a deep breath. Slowly an image began to form in my imagination.

I waited until the picture felt more real than the room around me, and then I started with the sky, sketching it with brilliant blues, and birds wheeling playfully in the clouds. I drew trees in the background: great friendly puffs of green leaves. I put grass in the foreground, dotted with gorse, broom and other wildflowers in yellows and purples. Steadily I worked towards the blank spot in the middle, where the golem would sit.

I was getting a bit nervous. So far I'd made a nice, calm landscape, but for this to work I had to imagine the golem being peaceful too, and capture that on paper. The image of its twisted face as it lunged at Euan and then fell kept popping into my head, blocking everything else out.

I looked at the spread of 54 pastels in front of me. I had no idea which ones to use. I'd made the golem from dark brown mud. Should I make my drawing true to life, or should I try changing its colour? Could I transform the golem's essence like that? After all, colours were just different vibrations of light. Mum had taught me that.

I shut my eyes again and let fear close in on me. The colours I saw were blacks and blood reds, a hideous puce and an evil group of greenish-browns. When I wondered what colour a fearful heart would be, I saw a heavy metallic grey: lead. I opened my eyes. The fear was gone. Michael had given me my answer.

The set of pastels Mum and Dad had given me for my birthday was the deluxe version, containing every colour including copper, silver and gold. The gold pastel was the only one in the whole box that the burglars hadn't touched, and it was still in perfect condition, its edges sharp and square because I'd had no reason to use it yet. Very carefully I prised it out of its slot. Using the gold pastel, I drew the golem sitting on a boulder smiling down at a semi-circle of rabbits, who were gazing back adoringly as they chewed their grass. For a finishing touch, I sat a tiny baby bunny on the golem's outstretched, golden hand.

I blew the pastel dust off the picture.

"Wow," said Euan.

I span round in my chair, wondering how long he'd been watching me.

"Great picture. I just hope it works." He looked a little pale. "Lucy's here. Your mum's grilling her about our science project, so we should probably rescue her before the lies fall apart."

"Whatever you do, don't be scared," said Lucy, as we walked through the undergrowth, following the same path we'd taken last night. "If you feel afraid, the golem will too, and it's kind of scary when it's scared."

"I'm fine," I said. "I told you, I know this will work."

"Well, at least one of us does," said Lucy.

"Do you think it's still down there?" Euan asked, hanging back as we approached the well. The hole seemed bigger than it was last night. I dropped onto my hands and knees and crawled as close as I dared go. It looked like giant fingers had raked the soil around the edge.

"It tried to get out," I said, getting to my feet and brushing the dirt off my knees. "But I don't know if it made it."

A baleful moan sounded behind us. The three of us whirled around and peered into the trees. I thought I could see a huge shadow hunched over on the ground about a hundred metres in. It had escaped. I swallowed the lump of fear that had formed in my throat.

"Quick, Lucy, get out your fiddle," I said.

Lucy fumbled with the clasps on her case, but she

got her instrument out. She placed it under her chin and started plucking the strings and fiddling with the tuning pegs.

"There's no time for that," said Euan.

"It's got to be in tune or it'll just sound sad," she said.

The golem moaned.

"Come on, play something," I said, my heart pounding in my chest as the monster staggered to its feet. The plan would work, but only if everyone did their part.

Flustered, Lucy drew her bow across the strings. A horrendous sound came out, like cats yowling in pain as they dragged their nails across a blackboard.

The golem roared.

"Hey, Lucy," said Euan, an edge of fear in his voice. "Do you know what happy sounds like?"

"I'm trying," she said. "I've never played for a monster before."

She started again. The jangled notes grew clearer and found their places. Soon she was playing a lively, bouncy jig. We watched, as the golem swayed in time to the music, but as it began to stumble towards us, Lucy's playing faltered.

The golem roared and its strides lengthened and quickened. I looked behind us and realised the mistake we'd made. I fought down the panic that threatened to overwhelm me: we were trapped between the golem and the well. *I am Edda the Brave*, I told myself. *I will not feed the golem with my fear.*

"Come on, Lucy, keep playing," said Euan. "You can do it."

White-faced, she gave him a small nod and shakily

resumed the tune. The golem slowed to a stop and began to sway again.

*I am Edda the Brave*, I told myself again. I took a deep breath, stepped forward and held up the picture. "Hey, Golem, I made you a present," I said. "It's a portrait. Would you like to see?"

My breath caught in my throat as the golem stumbled out of the tree cover. Lucy tripped over a note, but kept playing. The golem stopped and cocked its huge head to one side, its hollow eyes focusing on the paper in my hand. It stretched one long arm towards me, uncurling its fingers. I caught a whiff of earth, of decaying leaves and of small hidden things waiting for the warmth of spring to make them grow. It was a comforting smell and the last of my fear flowed away. The golem's skin was cold and rough against mine as I placed the picture in its hand.

"I made a drawing of what I wish for you," I said. "As your maker," I added, in case that would give my words more power. It stood so still, gazing down at the drawing, I thought for a moment that life had left it, but then it started to croon.

"Now, Euan," I whispered, stepping back.

Euan walked up to the giant, clutching the wire brush and chisel my dad had lent him as if they were a shield and a sword. He was barely taller than the creature's waist. His hand shook as he reached up to sweep away the symbols on its chest. The golem was so taken with my picture, it didn't seem to notice him at all. Once the creature's chest was bare, Euan tossed the brush on the ground. I saw his arm move, tracing the shape of a heart, but when he lowered the chisel and stepped back I couldn't see anything.

"You're going to have to go deeper than that," I whispered.

He looked at me, his eyes bright with fear in his pale, drawn face, but he nodded and raised the chisel again. This time the golem noticed him, its sunken eyes watched the chisel coming closer.

Lucy started playing louder and faster. It worked. The golem swung its head round to look at her, but then it started tapping its foot, shaking the ground, and I heard a clump of dirt cascade into the well behind us.

"Can you play something happy but more calm?" I asked.

She slowed the jig down and transformed it into a lullaby. The golem's foot stopped moving. It crooned again and looked back down at the picture.

Using the edge of the chisel, Euan cut deep into the golem's flesh. Slowly and carefully he drew the chisel up and around, the muscles in his arm straining as he etched a large heart into the golem's chest.

Euan looked at me again. This time I could see the heart clearly. I nodded and he stepped back to join us. Lucy let the music fade away.

The golem lifted its head and mewed questioningly.

I raised my arms to make sure I had its attention.

"Golem, as your maker, I release you. You are no longer needed to protect my house, my family, my friends or me. You are free."

A warm sunbeam from the setting sun cut through the woods, illuminating the golem's chest. The lines that Euan had carved started to glow. At first I thought it was a trick of the light, but when a cloud passed in front of the sun the heart grew even brighter, its colour shifting to the exact shade of the pastel I'd used to draw the golem. The heart flared once and faded, leaving just a hint of colour in the golem's skin: a golden glow.

The golem looked down at its chest, traced the outline of the heart with one of its thick fingers and made a low rumbling sound, like a cross between a purr and a landslide. The gash I'd given it for a mouth softened and the golem smiled down at us, then it turned and strode away, its huge feet scarcely making a sound on the forest floor.

## 23. CLOSED DOORS AND OPEN DOORS

The three of us ambled slowly up the path behind the wall, chattering happily about the amazing things we'd seen over the last two days. By the time we left the park it was getting late and Lucy had to rush home for dinner. Euan hurried off too, mumbling there was something he needed to do, but we all agreed to meet at school the next day and talk more about our adventures.

Dad was still cooking dinner when I came in the door, so I went to my room, took out my sketchbook and pastels and began to draw the scene in the woods. I drew Lucy playing her fiddle while Euan chiselled a heart on the chest of the massive golem, who was holding the picture I'd made. I drew myself facing the golem, my hand stretched towards it. As I gazed down at the finished sketch, I realised just how incredibly brave we'd all been and I felt a flood of pride.

That night I slept soundly, my dreams filled with fuzzy bunnies, golden sunsets and friendly giants made of earth. I woke the next morning feeling rested and excited all at the same time. I bolted down my breakfast and raced out the door, eager to see my friends, but hoping Michael would be there too. I wanted to tell him that I'd figured out how to turn lead into gold and to show him I wasn't a scared little mouse any more.

When I got to school, there was still no old-fashioned red bike in the rack and Euan and Lucy were nowhere to be seen. In fact, my two friends didn't arrive until just before the bell so I didn't get a chance to talk to them before class.

"Where is he?" I muttered, as I took my seat, annoyed that I actually missed Michael. In the end, he had helped me get over my fears.

"Where's who?" asked Lucy.

"Michael," I said. "As in *The*-Michael-Scot – 'I know how to make a golem and terrify people.'"

Lucy looked confused. "How to make a what?"

I sighed. Why was she acting so weird? "The boy who sits back there." I pivoted around in my chair to point, but in the place where Michael's desk used to be stood a tall potted palm, its leaves dull with a year's worth of dust.

"I don't understand," I said, a little louder than I meant to.

"Well, Edda," said Mrs Doak, "perhaps if you turned round and stopped talking, you'd understand better."

I did as I was told, but I couldn't focus on anything besides what had happened to Michael Scot – and why Lucy seemed to have forgotten him and the monster he'd helped me make.

"You really don't remember him?" I asked Lucy at lunchtime. "Tall, skinny, round glasses, dark hair that's always messy – called his diary *The Book of Might.*"

"You've been reading too much Harry Potter," said Lucy.

"Michael Scot is nothing like Harry Potter," I said.

"Are you all right?" asked Lucy.

"I'm fine," I said hotly. "You're the one who's lost her memory. Look, if Michael Scot never existed, how did I become friends with Euan?"

Lucy took a sip of her blackcurrant juice while she considered the question. "You stood up to him, so he stopped teasing you," she said finally. "And then you realised he wasn't so bad..." she trailed off, looking doubtful. We both watched Euan with his friends Murdo and George. They were being idiots as usual. "Actually, I never quite understood how you two became friends," finished Lucy.

"It was when I went to warn him about the golem..." I began.

"You used that word before. What is a golem?"

"The huge creature I made out of mud," I said. "The one you and Euan helped me to stop yesterday on Corstorphine Hill. You played your fiddle while Euan rubbed out the word on its chest – remember? Together we tamed a monster!" I told her the whole story. Lucy looked more and more concerned.

"You've really let your imagination run away with you this time," she said. "Do you have a fever? Maybe you should go and see the nurse."

I tried and tried but I couldn't convince her that Michael Scot or the golem existed, and by the time I'd finished talking to her, I was starting to doubt it myself. But if Michael and the golem didn't exist, did that mean Edda the Brave was also a figment of my imagination? I knew I'd changed. Hadn't I?

I walked Lucy to her house and then headed up Hillside Drive. I hadn't gone far when I heard a horrible screeching behind me. I turned around. Euan was cycling up the hill towards me, his bicycle weaving crazily from side to side. Every time his feet went round on the pedals, the bike protested.

"Hi," he called, taking his hand off the handlebars to give me a wave. The bike swerved alarmingly close to the edge of the road. "I came to show you my bike," he said, catching up with me and stopping.

"Your bike?" I said, unable to keep the disbelief out of my voice. "As in the one that got – uh – accidentally run over?" The picture that sprang from my memory was of a mangled, twisted knot of metal and tyres.

"Yeah," said Euan. "I took it to the second-hand place you talked about, to see if I could sell it for parts – it was a really expensive bike. They wouldn't buy it, but this guy showed me how to fix some stuff and he said I could use their tools as long as I do some volunteering. So..." With a flourish, he gestured towards the bike.

"You've been fixing it," I said.

"Yeah," said Euan, beaming with pride. "It still needs a lot of work – I wouldn't ride it to school yet or anywhere someone might see it, but it got me here."

"That's great," I said, taking it as a compliment that Euan was willing to show it to me before anyone else.

"I should get going," he said. "I have to hide it again before my brother gets home."

"Wait," I said. I had to know if he'd forgotten too. "I need to ask you something."

He shrugged. "Okay."

"This might sound a little crazy, but do you remember the kid in our class, Michael Scot?"

"Michael who?" he asked, looking genuinely puzzled. How could they both have forgotten everything we'd just been through? If Michael could escape people's notice, maybe he could wipe himself from their memories as well.

"Do you remember why we went into the park yesterday?" I asked Euan.

"Sure," said Euan. "You, me and Lucy had a science project to do."

That was always Michael's standard lie. "So what was our project on?" I asked.

"We had to..." Euan trailed off. He frowned, obviously puzzled, but then he shrugged. "Something too boring to bother remembering."

"What about the golem?" I asked.

"As in, 'My Precioussss'?" he said.

"No, that's not what I mean," I said with a sigh. "Never mind."

I watched him ride back down the hill, his bicycle wobbling precariously.

There was no science project. Michael had erased my friends' memories, I was certain of it, but could I prove it?

*

When I got home, both my parents were out, and there was a note on the fridge door saying they'd gone to look at houses in Morningside. My heart sank; Mum hadn't given up on moving.

I went to my room and pulled out my sketchbook. I turned to the picture I'd drawn last night of the scene in the woods. It was still there, and so was the edge where I'd torn off the drawing I'd given to the golem. I opened up my box of pastels. The gold one had been worn down along the top edge. It proved I'd made the pictures, but it didn't prove I'd made the golem.

Strictly speaking, I still wasn't allowed to go to the park on my own, but I had to find Michael. I decided if I took Henry with me, I wouldn't really be going by myself.

The sky was a deep, gorgeous blue and the wind was swishing lightly through the trees, making the leaves murmur softly together, as Henry and I passed through the gate. Henry immediately tried to turn towards the rabbit field, but I had different plans. I headed up the path that led to the tower, Henry following reluctantly behind me.

The closer we got to the tower, the lower Henry's tail drooped and the more he lagged behind. When the tower came into view, he started whining. I had to drag him the last ten metres.

"You're a good dog," I said to him. "You remember Michael, don't you?" He just looked at me with baleful eyes. As I pounded on the heavy, iron door, he hung back as far as his leash would allow.

There was no answer.

"Michael!" I shouted. "I need to see you."

An older man walked by with his dog and frowned at me. His dog was slinking along the far fence, avoiding the tower. I glared at the man and he kept walking.

As soon as he was out of sight I pounded on the door again. Henry whined and lay down, covering his face with his paws. I tried the door, but it was locked. I gave up. Michael either wasn't there or he didn't feel like talking to me. I was about to leave when I noticed a laminated sheet of paper taped to the side of the tower.

"Doors Open Day," it said. "Saturday, 25 September." That was this weekend.

I read the rest of the announcement with rising excitement. Apparently, Michael wasn't the only one with a key to the tower.

Over dinner, I listened with a lifting heart as Mum complained about the houses they'd looked at. None were as nice as this one and they all cost way too much.

"They're letting people into Corstorphine Hill Tower on Saturday," I told them, when Mum was finished. "We should go. You can see for miles from up there, all the way to the Wallace Monument. At least that's what I've heard," I added.

Saturday was a perfect autumn day, clear and sunny, and the trees of Corstorphine Hill were decked out in their yellow and gold finery as Mum, Dad and I walked along the path to the tower. As we came into the clearing that surrounded it I was surprised to see a long line of people snaking into the distance. At the base of the tower someone had set up an old wooden school desk and covered it with leaflets.

After what felt like a hundred years of shuffling forward then waiting, then shuffling forward again, we finally got to the front of the line. The man behind the desk wore a badge that said "Friends of Corstorphine Hill". He passed us one of the leaflets, which explained what could be seen from the top of the tower, and ushered us through the heavy door.

"It used to be the door for the Tolbooth Prison," I told my parents.

"Well, aren't you the font of knowledge, Mouse," said Dad, ruffling my hair.

Mum and Dad headed up the stairs, but there was something else I needed to do. I waited until my parents had disappeared from sight, then I slipped behind the spiral staircase and lifted the soiled mat that hid the trapdoor from view.

There was nothing underneath but the same thick stone slabs that covered the rest of the floor. I couldn't believe my eyes. I knew there was a secret chamber beneath the tower. I'd been down there. I'd smelled the strange herbs and powders. I'd stroked the stuffed owl. It had all felt too real to be a dream. Maybe the stones were just an illusion. I crouched down and ran my fingers over their surface. They felt like rocks: cold, smooth, hard, and way too heavy to be lifted.

"Edda, are you coming?" Mum called down, leaning over the railing above me.

"Yeah," I said, standing up and letting the mat fall back into place.

I climbed the stairs slowly, feeling confused and miserable. It seemed as though Lucy was right after all. The whole adventure had only taken place in my overactive imagination. There was no Edda the Brave. I was destined to be Edda the Mouse forever.

At the top of the stairs a woman with the same Friends of Corstorphine Hill badge held the door open for me. I stepped outside and immediately felt better. The little wind turbine Michael and I had made was still there, perched on the battlements, twirling merrily in the breeze. My adventures with Michael and the golem had happened, here was the proof. I was so happy I laughed out loud.

The woman followed my gaze. "Someone's science project," she said. "It's lovely, isn't it?"

I smiled and nodded, wondering what she'd say if I told her the truth.

I stayed up there a long time, looking out over the trees and houses towards the hills and the sea, trying to memorise it all. When I got back down, Mum and Dad were chatting with the man at the desk, who was holding a filled-in membership form and a five-pound note. As I listened to the adults natter on I began to smile. The man had convinced Mum to run an art course on the hill and he and Dad were hatching up a plan to hide a series of wooden sculptures around the woods. If there was one thing my parents could not resist, it was community art projects. It looked like we might be staying on Corstorphine Hill for a while longer.

We took the long way home, stopping to sit on a bench overlooking the city. "This place is called 'Rest and Be Thankful,"' said Mum, brandishing a handful of leaflets.

I leaned back and looked up at the clear blue sky, thinking about all the things I had to be thankful for: my friends, my parents, this wild place in the city, and the bungalow on the side of the hill, which I had a hunch I'd get to call home for many years to come.

There was just one more thing I needed to take care of. Michael, the boy alchemist, had vanished and he'd taken my friends' memories with him. He'd left my mind alone, at least for the time being, but I had to do something to make sure that no matter what happened I would never ever doubt I was Edda the Brave again. A smile spread across my face. I knew exactly what to do.

## 24. EDDA THE BRAVE

The next morning I got up early, wrote a note for my parents, who were still in bed, packed up my sketchbook and pastels and caught the bus to Princes Street.

I got off at The Mound in front of the big sandstone building that belonged to the Royal Scottish Academy of Art. I stood for a minute, admiring its tall columns and the huge stone sphinxes that crouched on its roof. Their human faces stared sweetly down at me but I wasn't fooled. Their lions' claws could shred a person with one swipe. I shuddered, hoping Michael never found a way to bring them to life.

I walked around the Royal Academy to the only slightly less splendid building behind it: the Scottish National Gallery. Inside were vast opulent rooms with high red walls and gold-framed pictures that had been painted hundreds of years ago in places like France, Holland and Italy. I strode quickly through these rooms. There was only one painting I wanted to see today and it was kept in the basement with all the other Scottish art. I took the stairs down two at a time and bounded through the door.

"No running," whispered the guard, shaking his head at me. It was hard to slow down when my heart was beating with excitement and my feet wanted to skip along the carpet, but I didn't want to get thrown out, so I did as I was told.

I threaded my way through a maze of small rooms and tight corridors until at last I was standing in front of it: *Una and the Lion*. If I'd been in charge, I would have given the painting a room of its own, or at least a wall, but here it was crowded round with other pictures. I'd got used to the reproduction on the cover of the sketchbook Lucy had given me, so I'd forgotten how vivid the colours were on the actual painting and how alive the girl and her wild-eyed lion looked. I sat on the leather bench in front of the painting, got out my sketchbook and pastels and started to copy it, only instead of drawing Una's face, I drew my own.

By the time I'd finished, it was past lunchtime and my stomach was rumbling. I looked down at my hands; they were smudged in a rainbow of colours. I took a tissue out of my pocket and did my best to wipe them clean.

"Nicely done," whispered the guard. He was the same one who'd told me not to run. "Are you entering it in the competition?" I nodded. "If I were a judge, you'd get my vote," he said and walked away.

My face flushed with pride. I carefully detached the page from my sketchbook and carried it down to the activities desk. The woman smiled as she took it from me. She typed my name, age and address into her computer and printed out a small tag, "Edda

Macdonald, 13", which she stuck to the bottom of my picture. I followed her down a long corridor, its walls covered by drawings other people had made, each one beautiful in its own way because it showed something of the person who had made it.

Using drawing pins, she stuck my picture onto a bit of blank corkboard. She returned to her desk, but I stayed for a moment longer gazing at it, feeling proud of what I'd done. I grinned to myself. There was a picture of me hanging in the National Gallery of Scotland. Not even Michael could say that.

When I got home, I could hear Dad hammering in his shed. I found Mum in the kitchen stirring something dark and chocolatey in a mixing bowl.

"Mouse, you're home," she said. "Did you have a good time?"

"Mm-hmm," I said. I hesitated. "Mum," I said finally. "There's something I need to say to you."

The seriousness of my voice caught her attention. She put the wooden spoon down, wiped her hands on her apron and came over to me. "Yes, what is it?"

"I'm thirteen years old now," I began, "and while I may be small, and I may sometimes make choices that end up being... well... bad, I am strong, and clever, and sometimes even brave." I took a deep breath. "So, I'd like you and Dad to stop calling me Mouse."

Mum's shoulders, which had crept towards her ears when I mentioned bad choices, relaxed again and she gave me one of her quirky half-smiles that made her look years younger.

"You're right," she said. "I'm sorry. Sometimes I forget how grown-up you are."

The oven buzzed to say it was ready. Mum went back to the counter and poured the batter into a cake tin.

"There's something else," I said to her back.

"I'm listening," she replied as she leaned down to put the tin in the oven. It smelled suspiciously like chocolate mousse cake.

I cleared my throat nervously. "I really like it here," I said finally. "I like my room. I like that I can see trees and squirrels from my bedroom window. I like Mr Campbell and taking Henry for walks. I've got friends here. This is my home and I don't want to move just because someone broke in and took our stuff."

Mum came over and put her hands on my shoulders. She stared me in the eyes. "You're not afraid to stay here?" she asked.

I shook my head.

"Me neither," said Mum, giving me a quick hug. "You should have seen the house prices in Morningside though. They were terrifying enough to scare a dolphin out of the water. We'll stay then, shall we?"

I nodded vigorously.

"At least for as long as I can stand teaching white-haired ladies in twinsets and pearls how to draw African violets."

"Mum," I said with a groan.

"Kidding," said Mum. "How could anyone get bored of that?"

I rolled my eyes. Mum would always be Mum, but I

wasn't worried. For now we were staying put. And the next time she got it into her head that we had to move, I'd find a way to stop her. I was Edda the Brave, fearless in the face of golems and bullies, able to dispose of housing ads in seconds flat, sculptor of life with pastel and mud alike.

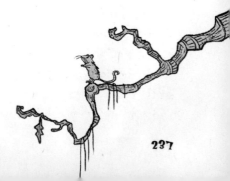

238

# THE GOLEM OF CORSTORPHINE HILL

Our garden is no longer a graveyard for small animals, and the "moles" seem to have moved elsewhere. There are still days when I feel scared and small, but when that happens I sneak off to a clearing in the woods of Corstorphine Hill and I lie in a large, monster-shaped hollow in the ground. After I've lain there for a few minutes, gazing up at the tops of the trees, taking slow, deep breaths of fresh hilltop air, I remember that love is the opposite of fear and that I have always been and always will be Edda the Brave.

Sometimes, late at night, I wake up to a familiar sound – *thumpety-thump, thumpety-thump-thump-thump* – and for a moment my heart starts to beat faster. But then I picture the golem dancing amongst the trees. I imagine that on days when he feels his heart grown cold and hard and full of spines and cobwebs again, he trundles down to a meadow on the sunny side of the hill. And there he sits as still as a boulder for days on end, while wind-blown grass seeds take root in his dirt skin and fluffy white-tailed bunnies tickle his feet. Then he remembers he has nothing to fear: he is and always will be part of Corstorphine Hill.